I0563270

Legacy of

Dragonwand

Book VII

By Daniel Peyton

Legacy of

Dragonwand

Book VII

By Daniel Peyton

Cosby Media Productions

Entertaining the Mind, and Inspiring the Soul

Cosby Media Productions
Entertaining the Mind and Inspiring the Soul

Legacy of Dragonwand Book VII

Copyright © 2025 by Daniel Peyton. All rights reserved.
No part of this publication may be reproduced, stored in a retrieval system or transmitted in any way by any means, electronic, mechanical, photocopy, recording or otherwise without the prior permission of the author except as provided by USA copyright law.
The opinions expressed by the author are not necessarily those of Cosby Media Productions.

Published by Cosby Media Productions, Inc.
Atlanta, Georgia

www.cosbymediaproductions.com
Contact Information: info@cosbymediaproductions.com

First Edition, June 2025
Paperback: **ISBN: 979-8-89965-076-5**

Cover Art: Cosby Media Productions

Editor: CMP

Published in the United States of America

TABLE OF CONTENTS

CHAPTER 1: DARKENING DAWN

MARKUS stood in the field, straining as he reached out. "MY WAND! WHERE'S MY WAND!" He tried again and again to summon his Dragonwand. Finally, it made sense. There was only one other person who could possibly have any power over his wand. His hand fell, and he felt a strange numbness in his chest. "Steffen...why did you do it?" He watched in the darkness of the night, seeing that Korvarsk and Steffen were long gone.

A huge thud shook the ground, causing Markus to topple over. He glanced back and saw that Donna had arrived, sprawled on the ground in a rather undignified manner.

"How do you make it look so easy?" she asked as she attempted to shake off her crash landing.

Markus got up. A fierce sorrow in his voice trickled out as he said, "It's too late. We lost him."

She transformed, her Dragonwand in her hand. "Damn! I'm going to skin that snake alive!" She then turned on Markus. "Why didn't you stop him? You were closer."

Markus held out his hands, revealing the lack of any tool."I tried. For some reason, Steffen prevented me from following."

"Why? For that matter, how?"

Markus shook his head. "I don't know why," he said softly. "Come on, you have to fly us back to Thendor. We need to figure this out."

She held up her Dragonwand, "I can go after them. He might have some kind of control over your wand, but he doesn't have any power over mine."

"No. You can't."

Donna shot him a vicious smile, like she was about to feast on his soul for stopping her. "Try me."

"And just what will you do? You barely know how to fly as a Dragon. Korvarsk has it mastered. Today, we lost Steffen, we can't lose you as well. We have to go back and figure this out, come up with a plan to combat this."

Donna fumed for a moment, her eyes lingering in the direction Korvarsk flew. After letting her fury subside, she said, "You're right. We have to do this logically. Flying headlong into a situation I know nothing about is foolish." She swiped her Dragonwand in the air and turned into her new second form.

For the first time, Markus got onto the back of another Dragon and flew. He sensed that Donna had a million questions; everyone would when he returned. He just didn't have the answers. The whole time he flew, he considered what had just transpired. Why would Steffen do that? What did Korvarsk, or that horrible Dark Lady, want with him? And what was he going to do next?

***

Steffen was dropped onto the ground, and a huge claw pressed on him. He gasped in the breath that had been knocked out of him. Korvarsk landed, keeping Steffen under one foot. Steffen wheezed and gasped to keep breathing. "Where are we?"

"Look." Korvarsk gestured with his head.

Steffen tipped his head up, making the world look upside down. He could see the desolate wasteland and many swarms of various dark creatures. Near them was the ancient wrecked ship. "You brought me back here? So, you're going to seal me in there like they sealed you."

Korvarsk laughed heartily. "What poetic justice that would be. But, alas, I need you with me. When I'm done, you will be dead, and I will be perfect."

"You know I can't be killed," Steffen retorted.

Korvarsk looked down at his captive. "The power that granted you that tattoo was matched by its perfect opposite. You know that. Just as a diamond can carve another diamond, so can the Pearl damage you." He looked up and shouted, "KELLEN! COME TO ME!" The booming voice stirred the shadow creatures; some seemed eager and energized by it, while others scurried away.

"Who's Kellen?" Steffen glanced around as much as he could from his pinned position.

A small man came out of the wreck in a short time, holding the Dark Pearl. It was high in his hands as he presented it. "My lady! I have saved you."

Korvarsk reverted to his Shlan form. Steffen was released from the claw and gradually rose to his feet. The Shlan rolled his shoulders and appeared as though he were in pain for a moment. A slithery dark mist seeped out of his body. The mist congealed into the form of a woman.

Kellen held the Pearl toward Steffen and forced him back against the ground. An invisible force pushed him so hard that the hard earth beneath him cracked. "You will not stand," Kellen proclaimed proudly.

The Dark Lady spoke to Korvarsk. "Retrieve his accursed wand."

"Yes, my lady." Korvarsk was again bewitched by the darkness placed in his mind. He leaned over and glared at Steffen. "Your wand!" He held out his hand.

Steffen grunted and groaned as he was still being pressed. "I...can't give it to you."

Korvarsk cast a simple electricity spell at Steffen. The crackling power hit Steffen's body and then rebound at Korvask who screeched when it shocked him.

"Don't be an idiot!" The Dark Lady shrilly stated. "Basic magic doesn't do much to him."

Korvarsk, enraged by his own injuring of himself, screamed at Steffen, "GIVE IT TO ME NOW!"

Steffen coughed and breathed shallowly before he said, "I...I don't have it. I lost it back in Thendor."

The Dark Lady put a hand on Korvarsk's shoulder, preventing him from losing his temper. "Steffen may be many things, but he is no liar. No matter, without his wand, he must truly abide by his agreement. He can't do much against us now."

"What now, my lady?" Kellen asked.

She moved her hand from Korvarsk's shoulder to his face, brushing the rough scales around his chin. "Now, my pets, we build a house fit for a queen. Kellen, the Dragonwand core." her left hand was held out, awaiting her prize.

Kellen shifted the Pearl to one hand, keeping Steffen down. With his free hand, he produced the glowing blue raindrop core. He placed it in her hand and then backed up.

"You can't use that," Steffen wheezed. "It will not respond to you. You must know that by now."

She laughed softly. "I know as much about these cores as you—perhaps more. I watched them be born, and I saw them in use. I've corrupted and controlled the minds of several Dragons over the years."

"And none of that makes any difference. What I am saying is still true. That core is worthless to you," Steffen said.

She knelt, face to face with him. "Don't be so certain. You see, you had time to learn and grow during these years, and I did too. I corrupted and controlled some Dragons, but when you banished me, they would regain their senses. I could never truly control them like I can wizards. I can't curse them like regular humans. I can't even lead them to death like other magical creatures in this world. Why? Because their cores were crafted through the magic of light. Purity. This is why you're so sure that each core's choice of a bearer is good, because if that person has any evil intentions, the core would never accept them."

Steffen did not hide the worry in his eyes right now. "Why are you telling me this?"

"Because I discovered that all I needed was to tap into light, twist it to my will, and through that, I could finally harness a Dragonwand core, eventually making it my heart. I won't create a new Dragonwand; I will create a new being of ultimate, ageless power. And I will not be just darkness; I will also be twisted light. Nothing will stand against me." She reached over and placed her hand on his tattoo. "And, as it happens, I have the most powerful source of light there is... you." Drawing her hand up, magic followed from his tattoo like a silky smoke wrapping around her fingertips. The light from his tattoo and the mist bathed the area around them with blinding brilliance. Kellen gagged and fell back while Korvarsk dropped to one knee, holding his chest. They both grunted and gasped as the agony ripped at them. The Dark Lady held a pained look in her eyes and her jaw clenched hard, yet she maintained a wicked smile at the actions she took.

"Please, stop. My lady. It burns." Korvarsk held up his hands, blocking the light.

"No. You can stand the pain. I am not finished. This would have been easier had your little boy not purified my beautiful taint. My strength might be dwindling, but it is not gone." Still holding that misty light, she whispered into the air. Threads of black darkness cut into the light, dimming it. The needle-like shards of darkness met Steffen's arm and he let out a horrible cry. "Now, now, my darling, this is only the beginning. The pain will increase." Reaching up, she pulled that corrupted light to the Dragonwand core. The power connected and began to stream into the core. She stood for a long time, allowing the drain of magic to continue. Steffen was inconsolably yelling the whole time.

"Does it not hurt you, my lady?" Kellen asked while he, too, covered his eyes from the light.

"It is excruciating like nothing I've truly experienced," she said with the core near her eager eyes. "Perfect pain; I relish such torture." Suddenly, she swiped her hand through the stream and cut it off. Steffen flopped his head against the ground, breathing hard as he recovered from that experience. The Dark Lady continued to stare at the core, watching the beautiful blue object now filled with flecks of black. While admiring the corrupted Dragonwand core, she said, "And, when I've drawn all the light out of you, you will no longer be immune to darkness. I will taint your soul, and you will finally be mine. I will have your heart. Oh, your soul will be dead, but your body will still work, a drone to serve the queen."

Korvarsk crept forward, afraid to get too close for fear of going through another experience like that. "Is it done? Is it ready for you to use?"

"Hardly," she answered, finally lowering it. "It has only begun. It will take time."

Kellen asked, "Why stop, my lady? We have what you desire to become a goddess."

With a satisfied smile at his description, she said, "Trust in me. I know what is best. This takes time. If I were to take it all from him now, he would die in the process. The light would be incomplete. Yet, do not despair, my precious pets, we will not simply bide out rim. I can harness some strength from it. Such a glorious abomination gives me power."

"Power...to do what?" Kellen asked.

She smiled and held up her hand. "This."

The ground rumbled for a moment, and then it vibrated as a crunching sound got louder and louder. Suddenly, a large spire broke through the earth and grew toward the sky. Then another and another. The spires grew larger and wider as they became towers.

Soon, walls came up with the towers, connecting them and forming the shape of a building. The ground directly beneath the gathering lifted, and the dirt blew away. Instead of sand, dirt, and rocks, they were standing on a solid floor. The towers and walls grew around them, connecting and forming into a vast courtroom.

Everything was made of solid black obsidian glass. The towers and pillars were lined with ornate spikes, and much filigree was carved into the stone. The floor had a cut pattern that formed a Dragon as large as this enormous room.

The whole time this place was forming, it rattled and shook; the sounds were deafening. Both Korvarsk and Kellen had to work to keep their balance. Steffen rolled around a bit before he stopped himself; he didn't even try to stand during this.

Finally, everything halted all at once.

A long silence enveloped them as they gazed at this incredible place. The courtroom featured massive open windows that overlooked the vast northern wastelands. Dark flying creatures swooped by, screeching and crying out. Far below, hordes of darkness gathered at the base of this ominous palace, drawn in by the powerful energy radiating from every stone.

Finally, Korvarsk asked, "Is it finished?"

"Not quite," the Dark Lady said and walked toward the back of the room. Stopping near the tall wall, she turned and then snapped her fingers. An amazing throne formed from the floor. It was wicked-looking, with even more ornate designs and cut figures of dragons on it. Like the rest of this place, it was solid black. Taking a gentle seat on the throne, she caressed the arm. "Now, it is complete."

"What now, my lady?" Kellen asked.

Her gaze fell on Steffen as he got to his feet. "Now, I regain my strength. I will become incredibly powerful as I corrupt the Dragonwand core and claim it for myself. However, I need more strength, I need more taint. My darkness feeds on corruption. You will go and spread taint to Gallenor, my loyal champion." She turned to Korvarsk. "Bring them to their knees."

"I will take great pleasure in doing this." He smiled insidiously.

"As for you, my dear beloved..." She held up her hand, and huge chains materialized from the pillars. Then, she flew through the room. They wrapped around Steffen and fastened themselves against five of the pillars. He was lifted in the air and secured tightly.

He struggled but then yelled in pain again. "What is this?"

"Pure darkness. Formed from a thousand years of waiting. Yes, my poor, diluted fool. You Dragons thought you could bind me in that damned shipwreck, and I would be weak. No. I crafted the most wonderful darkness in there. I built a storeroom of hatred and evil. With enough power you just provided me, I could weave and spin that wicked darkness into this."

Steffen frowned. "But, you must garner the evil from others. You cannot make it yourself."

Standing from her throne, she strolled through the room toward him. "Oh, but I am never truly alone. I am not just the Pearl of Darkness. You know this...my precious fool. You know this...BETTER THAN ANYONE!" Standing before him, she transformed into the feline woman he once loved. A deep rage was in the fury of her eyes as she snarled at him.

He gasped and whispered, "Alieth...oh, what have I done?"

Holding up the Dragonwand core, she made it float before him. Then she tapped his tattoo again and harnessed the light in him. The screams of agony from him echoed throughout this palace of pure hate.

***

A dark, formless void spread out around Markus. How he got here, or where this was, remained a mystery to him. The air was heavy, like a thick fog pressed down on him. The attempt to call his Dragonwand to his hand was futile. All he could do was cast a flame spell to provide a modicum of light, but that, too, seemed reduced by this utter darkness.

"Hello?" He called out, his voice echoing throughout this realm.

"Markus." The pained and distant voice of Steffen came to him.

Markus moved forward, unable to judge distance in this inky darkness. "Steffen! Where are you?"

"Markus, please, don't come," Steffen's weak voice floated on the air.

Markus stopped moving. He turned around twice. "But, I want to help you. I have to save you."

"You cannot save me." Suddenly, the voice was behind him.

Markus turned around, shocked to find Steffen on the ground, kneeling with his head bowed. "Steffen, what happened? Where are you?"

"I...I can't manage this for long." His breath seized and he strained all his muscles for a moment before letting out a soft, low groan.

Markus came down to the ground and held Steffen by the shoulders. "Tell me what to do? Where I can find you, help you."

"Gah!" Steffen tensed, held his breath momentarily, and finally took in short, hard breaths. "No. Please, don't come. You can't come to me. It's too dangerous."

"I can help. I'm not weak. I can save you." Markus attempted to lift Steffen so that he would look at him.

Steffen fought through the pain again and said, "No. She... gah... she is mistaken. She wanted me, but I couldn't help her any longer. She needs you to complete her work. You have the light. If you come, she will extract it from you... like... she is trying... with me." He cringed and bent over until his head touched the ground.

"The light? I don't understand. Just tell me where you are!"

Steffen whispered, "I can't. You are precious to me, my family. Hold to what is good in your heart and the evil in this world will never win. I... I have to die, that is the only way this can end."

"What? Please, something is wrong here. You need me."

"Please listen to me!" Steffen yelled from his prone position. "I don't matter; this is all my fault. I have to endure this long enough for you to get away. Far away, where she can't find you."

"I'm not going anywhere else. I have to save you!" Markus was getting angry.

Steffen lurched up and grabbed Markus by the hands, tears streaming down his face, his eyes wide with intensity. "Listen to me! Please, just listen. Her plans will ultimately fail again, as they have before; she will corrupt this land but lose her power without the light to harness for the core. Eventually, she will retreat into the Pearl and be lost for another thousand years, maybe even longer. If you come, she could extract from you what she desires, and then all life in the entire world will perish. Darkness will consume everything."

"But..."

Steffen pulled Markus close, wrapping his arms around him like a loving parent. "I lost Tolen when he chose to fight this; I can't lose you. You're all that matters to me now. I would give my life to save yours. Please, just do as I say and promise you won't try to rescue me. I'm not worth it."

Markus held Steffen in return. "I...I promise."

Steffen did not let go; he whispered, "I love you, Tolen," and vanished.

The feeling of Steffen's arms around him lingered as Markus slowly opened his eyes to the real world. After a second of blurriness, he made out the sight of a stone ceiling and a candelabra on a chest of drawers in the corner. The smell of goose down hit his nose and he realized his head was resting on a soft pillow.

"Where am I?" He pushed himself up and looked around.

He was in a small guest room in the palace. Someone had put his belongings there.

"How did I get in here?" he asked. The last thing he recalled was that he was riding Donna back to Thendor. He didn't remember arriving, just drifting off. His last memories slowly returned. He had been riding Donna's dragon-form back to Thendor when a strange tiredness grabbed him and he blacked out. "Was I just tired, or was that Steffen reaching out to my mind?" He asked himself.

The latch on the door moved, and he sat up to see who was coming in. The door opened and Treb came in, carrying his baby. In a hushed voice, Treb said, "Oh, good, you're awake."

Markus rubbed his eyes. "How long have I been asleep?"

"About eight hours. It's nearly lunchtime. Man, you're heavier than you look."

Markus frowned. "What?"

14

"When Donna got back with you, I carried you into this room and put you to bed."

"Oh, um... thanks."

Treb cocked his head and asked, "Are you crying?"

Markus reached up and brushed his hand across his face. There were tears in his eyes, and his cheeks were both damp. Wiping his eyes, he nodded. "I guess I have been. I...it's been difficult these past few days." He didn't want to tell Treb what he had experienced in his dream.

"We've all been through a lot over these past few days. But you've had it bad. Even I got to sleep while waiting outside Kiin's room."

Markus asked, "How is Kiin?"

Treb smiled at his baby, snuggled against his furry chest. "She's doing well. Crystal has worked hard to help heal people. Some of the purified wizards have been able to lend a hand, and things are looking better for those who survived the ordeal."

"She's a brilliant wizard," Markus said.

Treb carefully walked over to the box of stuff resting on a table in the corner. He gently rocked as he moved to keep his baby from waking, shuffling through the stuff.

"What are you doing?" Markus asked, a little nervous about Treb rifling through his belongings.

"I'm looking for something."

"Um, that's my stuff." Markus sat up on the side of his bed, only to realize he was still dressed in his wizarding robes, which meant no one had changed his clothes for him to sleep in.

"I know. It was brought here, and I...let's see...ah, here it is." Treb pulled out the box with the engagement necklace and brought it over to Markus.

Markus stiffened slightly, his heart raced faster, and a cold sweat broke across his body. "What are you doing with that?"

Treb handed it to Markus, who opened it to ensure it was still safely inside. The last time he saw it was before he was arrested in the Port of Pearls. Treb pointed at the opened necklace. "I haven't seen one like that in a long time. But I know what that is."

"That... uh... you know... There was this vendor in the Port of Pearls who had that. I thought it was pretty. And... " Not an once of wisdom from his vast memory aided him in this moment.

Treb gave Markus a plain look. "I'm well aware what this is. This is a Rakki traditional engagement necklace. And, I know you know that."

Markus gazed at the necklace, knowing that he had to be completely honest now. "It's for Crystal." Looking up at Treb with worried eyes, he said, "And?"

Treb gently rocked his baby back and forth. "A year ago, I would have been incensed by that. I never thought you were good enough for my little Crystal. Even after you saved Gallenor, I thought you just weren't right for her. I know I was being overprotective, but I also recognized that you were a bit ambitious and headstrong, which I didn't believe was suitable for her."

"But?" Markus wasn't sure where he was heading with this.

"But watching her grow and become a brilliant wizard has changed my mind. She was so meek and insecure as a child. She loved to study and work in the corner of our village's healing hut. She thought little of her abilities and only wished for her parents to be around so she could hide in their shadows. You brought out a strength in her that makes me happy. She is anything but timid now, smarter than ever...which is impressive, and she can more than keep up with you."

Markus nodded. "She goes right past me some days."

"True. This tells me you've brought her the confidence she lacked. I want you to know I'm happy you're ready for this next step. I know she is. She can have no better a husband than you."

Markus closed the box. "You know, I was terrified of telling you about this. I even thought about suggesting she and I eloped so we could tell you after we were officially married."

Treb pestered him. "You, the Mighty Lord Dragon, afraid of little me?"

"Yes," Markus replied. "But I knew she would never allow that. She would want your blessing just as much as her father's."

"You have mine, and I'm sure Shio will be pleased to give you his daughter. Just promise me that you'll keep her safe."

Markus's lightened mood faded. "I will do everything I can to ensure she is safe."

Treb frowned at Markus, "Something wrong?"

"It's nothing."

The door to the room opened, and a servant poked his head in. He whispered to Treb, "Is the Lord Dragon awake? Oh, Lord Dragon, your presence is requested in the courtroom immediately."

Markus stood from his bed. "Thank you." The servant rushed off.

Treb headed for the door but was stopped by Markus, who held his arm. "What? Did you need something else?"

Markus leaned in and gazed down at the sleeping baby girl. She had fluffy white fur and the cutest little wet nose. "I haven't had a chance to really see her. She's beautiful."

Treb beamed with pride. "Yes, I can't wait to see what color her fur turns out to be. I hope she looks like her mother."

"What's her name?"

"She'll be named during a naming ceremony after her ninetieth day."

Markus nodded. "That's right, Crystal told me about that. Rakki don't name their children for three months. Are Rakki babies always pure white when they're born?"

"Not often; in fact, I don't think I've ever seen one this white. Most of the time, they are dingy brown or gray. But that only makes her more special." He cooed over his child.

"I'm so happy for you and Kiin. She has the best parents."

Treb said, "Fortunately, we got some practice by taking care of Crystal. Though, an infant will require a new set of skills. Now, I will take her to the old candle maker."

"The candle maker?"

"She is watching the children of people who are recovering or working on the current situation. Everyone is doing something to help." Treb walked on down the corridor.

Markus straightened his wrinkled robes and headed out the door.

As Markus entered the courtroom, he noticed the palace was almost entirely empty. There were no people lying on the ground, and no doctors or nurses were working; only a few guards and some courtiers hurried about. Kellus was talking to Norl, while someone sat in a chair near the throne. Markus couldn't see the man in the chair.

Norl noticed Markus first. "Ah, Markus. Good. I see that you've rested."

Markus nodded once. "Yes. I'm a little upset you let me sleep for so long. There is much to do."

Suddenly, Lord Flavian's voice spoke. "We've taken care of many things while you slept. A rested mind is far more useful than an overtaxed one."

Kellus stepped aside to reveal that Lord Flavian was seated in the chair. Markus bowed respectfully to the governor. "My Lord, I'm glad to see you up. How are you feeling?"

Flavian bowed his head to Markus. "I'm doing well now that I'm no longer tainted."

Kellus said, "Lord Flavian has been doing exceptionally well. He has taken charge effectively and helped coordinate the city during this time. The hospital has admitted many of the seriously wounded; he ordered the community centers to be opened as healing areas so that the sick wouldn't be lying around the palace. He even helped organize the guard rotation to handle the Shlan legions currently surrounding the city."

Flavian remarked, "Lord Kellus and his men have also done an excellent job of rounding up the Shlan warriors and monitoring the situation. Without the Rakki presence, we would have very little security right now."

Markus again bowed his head to them. "You have acted wisely during this event. Thank you."

"We didn't call you here to boast about our success," Norl said. "We have issues to address."

Markus frowned. "What is that?"

Flavian asked, "Master Donna explained what little she knew about that evil Dragon and the man he stole. But, we are still working on hardly any information."

Markus said, "Korvarsk is being controlled by that evil darkness that Steffen told you about before. The Dark Lady wanted him for something."

Kellus asked, "Are we in danger? Is this Dark Lady planning another attack?"

"I can't say exactly what she is up to. But I do not believe we are in immediate danger yet. I will have to give this thought and consider all my ancient wisdom before I have any suggestions on how to proceed. However, as I said, I believe we are safe for now."

"What of the Shlan?" Norl asked.

"The purification spell has broken her control over the Shlan king and his forces."

"Speaking of the Shlan." Flavian clapped his hands. "Bring them in!" He then said to Norl, "Go gather the representatives."

Markus waited while the palace doors were opened, and a team of Rakki warriors escorted Lord Shashla'yar and his commanders into the throne room. Their hands were bound, and they had swords pointed at them.

Norl returned from his quick exit, bringing the race representatives with him. Three of the four stood with Flavian,

Kellus, and Markus, while the Shlan representative stood with her people.

Shashla'yar said something to his people, and they all got on their knees, even the representative. Their heads were low, and they were quiet.

Flavian spoke, "It is time we deal with the treasonous acts of..."

"Stand!" Markus interrupted.

Everyone stopped and looked at him with shocked expressions, even the Shlan. Kellus frowned. "What did you say?"

Markus walked over, summoned his Dragonwand, and then used it to dissolve the bindings on Shashla'yar's hands. He then said it again, "Stand, all of you."

There was much commotion among the non-Shlan in the room while the Shlan stood back up, confused and almost worried.

Flavian finally asked, "What are you doing?"

"I'm going to see that this doesn't go wrong."

Norl cleared his throat and said, "Lord Dragon, you are not in authority to judge or prescribe punishment at this time. Your title is that of advisor, not ruler."

"That may be. But, I ask that the acting ruling body of this nation heeds my ancient wisdom in this case. Please, listen to me before you continue with your judgment."

Flavian nodded, "Speak, Lord Dragon. The floor is yours."

Markus turned and walked through the crowd in the middle of the room. "Twice, the evil darkness has set nations against each other. Twice she has crippled and destroyed powerful lands. We are Gallenor, a land united by trust and peace. I know that the Shlan acted treacherously in our eyes, but I understand the evil behind it. I will not allow anyone in this room who is not guilty, to kneel in submission to another. The Shlan are a proud people who were misled. They acted only to protect themselves from perceived threats."

Lord Flavian asked, "How do you know this? Do you now read minds?"

Markus looked directly at Shashla'yar. "My best friend is Korvarsk, and his father is close to me. Hlarsk came to us, escaping your land to prevent this disaster. He told me the truth; he told me what was happening and that the Heart of Darkness used you, like so many before you. I will not allow the darkness to drive wedges between anyone in this nation. We need the Shlan as much as we need the Rakki, Momar, or humans."

Lord Norl asked, "What did Hlarsk tell you that would justify their actions? Bad influence is not an excuse for treason."

Markus looked at Shashla'yar. "He told me that the objective was not to attack or take power but to apprehend me. Their ultimate goal was not just the security of the Shlan but of the nation. I find no fault in their intentions; their plan was to do so peacefully first. Only through clever machinations by a three-thousand-year-old villain were they led to the point of staging an attack on this city. I say they acted in accordance with the law, for their goal was the safety of Gallenor."

Norl gave Shashla'yar a grim glance. "Why are you so certain the Shlan's desire to rule again did not fuel their plans? There have been several occasions over the centuries that the Shlan grabbed opportunities to overthrow Thendor to return to the Shlan Empire, though each time they failed."

Shashla'yar opened his mouth, his eyes flared in rage and a deep breath ready to exhale a counter argument. However, Markus stopped him with a single hand held up. "I know the history. I'm fully aware that the Shlan have had moments of desire to return to leadership of this nation. However, I know and trust Lord Shashla'yar. His expressed desire for community among all kinds in this land has been clear and honest. And, there is another history to consider. The evil behind all of this has used this same hatred and bigotry to overthrow entire lands. Seeding mistrust and chaos is her greatest weapon. Let us not forget that. The Shlan have been good allies and friends of this nation for a long time. The Darkness has ever always been a rabid wolf eager to spread fear into her prey. I trust the Shlan."

Kellus answered, "What say you, Lord Shashla'yar?"

Shashla'yar cleared his throat and said, "I will not deny that my people attacked. But, I know that until thisss city wasss purified, my thoughtsss had become darker and angrier. When the purification happened, a fog lifted from me. I no longer wasss ssso angry." He bowed his head. "We will help fix thisss. We only want peace with our neighborsss in Gallenor."

"LET GO OF ME! DON'T YOU KNOW WHO I AM!" The belligerent voice of Baron Thorne came up the steps of the palace.

Donna came in, holding the Baron by the back of his shirt. "Stop bellyaching; you whine worse than a youngling." She shoved him into the room. Everyone gawked at this display. She smiled at Markus. "Oh, you're up. Good. Look who I found." Just then, she noticed everyone. "Oops, I interrupted something, didn't I?"

"Your timing is perfect," Markus commented.

Baron Thorne dusted himself off and straightened out his clothes. "How dare you treat me like this. I'm the future King of Gallenor!"

Donna summoned her Dragonwand and pointed it at the Baron threateningly to prevent him from running for it. "I found this one outside the city, attempting to bribe a Rakki guard to keep quiet about his arrival."

Kellus took a step forward. "Baron Thorne, how nice to see you."

"Kellus." Thorne sneered at his old opponent. "Look, I don't know what the big deal is. I have an estate in this city. I was not trying to bribe anyone; this woman is lying. I am a member of the royal house, a future king, and not someone to push around. Now, will someone tell me what is going on?"

Kellus was about to reply when Markus kindly held up his hand to interrupt. "No need to lie, Baron. I know what you've been up to."

"Up to? Now what is this boy accusing me of? I demand..."

"ENOUGH!" Shashla'yar yelled. "This man was part of the conspiracy."

"How dare you!" Thorne retorted with false indignation. "I was brainwashed by the Shlan Korvarsk. He used some evil dragon magic on me or something."

Markus tapped the end of his Dragonwand against the floor, producing a rumbling crack of thunder that echoed through the courtroom, effectively capturing the attention of everyone present. "No more from you."

"But.."

Markus had a fire in his eyes that shut the Baron up. He turned to Flavian. "According to the Constitutional Concordant, when there is a serious conflict between the races, the Lords must sit and talk. I believe this situation fits that well enough. I will recommend to this court that Lords Kellus, Flavian, and Shashla'yar be allowed to agree on how to proceed. I also recommend that Representative Amber be present on behalf of the Momar." He looked at Norl.

Norl turned to the race representatives, and they spoke very briefly. Then, he returned with a smile. "This is acceptable."

Flavian spoke. "But, Lord Dragon, I am not a race Lord, just a governor. The human race lord was the sitting king. We do have have that."

Markus said, "I believe a proxy is allowed."

"It is," Norl added.

Amber, the Momar representative, quickly said, "I nominate Governor Flavian o the Port o Pearls ta be proxy for race representative o the humans."

Norl nodded, and the other representatives gave their approval. Norl answered, "It is acceptable."

"I will do my best," Flavian replied humbly.

With that, the group left the room for one of the meeting areas. The Shlan commanders were escorted out of the court, now free of bondage.

Donna asked, "What about this one?" She glared at Baron Thorne.

He held up his hands and gave off an innocent smile. "You must believe me. I was cursed or something. I didn't mean to do what I did."

Markus drew dangerously close to the Baron, staring him in the eyes with a deep penetrating look.

The Baron coughed and said, "What are you doing?"

Donna asked, "Yeah, what are you doing?"

Markus said, "I can sense something changed in Shashla'yar. It is the same feeling I had when you were cleansed of the taint. A darkness that is gone. In this one, the feeling in him has not changed. He didn't have the darkness in him to begin with. What you did, you did without influence other than the promise of power."

"Wait a minute. You can't just stare me in the eye and then decide my fate!"

Markus gently yet firmly, gripped the front of his stuffed shirt, pulling him almost off the ground. "You are lucky I'm not the villain you and your kind have painted me as. Right now, I want to throw you into the deepest part of the ocean and let the Leviathan's children devour you. But I won't. I'm going to give you the same lavish accommodations you offered me while you tried to convict me." He shoved the Baron to one of the guards. "Put him in a cell and keep him there."

"Yes, Lord Dragon." The guard quickly took the rattled Baron away.

Donna approached with a hint of caution in her step. "Um, that was interesting. I don't think I've ever seen you quite that angry."

Markus still showed some of that anger on his face. "That man is allied with the Dark Heart, the same Dark Heart that has taken my best friend and now Steffen. He chose to be evil."

"I know. So, what are we going to do about it? I say..."

"Nothing," Markus stated coldly.

Donna was taken aback, her eyes wide and mouth open. "You...but...what did you say?"

Markus walked onward toward the large doors. "I said we're going to do nothing about this. Right now, we will help the people here recover, that's all."

Donna wanted to say much more right then, but Markus simply walked away, leaving her dumbfounded.

CHAPTER 2: THE TAINT SPREADS

STILLWATER was as lively as ever. Reports of the strange happenings at Thendor had only just begun to trickle into town. If the Royal Guard outpost hadn't doubled its numbers on the streets, people wouldn't have been asking questions. The official responses to any questions were vague, but enough to sate any concerns.

Tasha set up her booth today and was ready to sell her potions to the usual customers. Since Donna left the shop, she has embraced the life of a potion maker with gusto. Although she couldn't make magical potions like Donna, she was proficient in making the day-to-day items that people needed.

An elderly woman stood in front of the booth, gazing at a bottle of yellow liquid. "Is this a hearing potion?"

Tasha nodded. "Yes, that's for hearing."

"I didn't say I lost my earring. I need a hearing potion," the old woman replied.

"I said that's a hearing potion."

"You say it tastes like herring?"

With a sigh, Tasha grabbed a piece of parchment and wrote on it. She then presented it to the customer.

"Oh, why didn't you mention that earlier? I'll take two bottles." The woman fished out a small handful of silver coins and paid for the potion that was supposed to help ease some of her troubles.

Tasha watched the woman walk away, chuckling to herself about that crazy conversation. Soon, she would have Mrs. Tarn come by for her regular order of spirit remover for her husband.

Tasha had just bent down to pick up a tray of fresh bottles of bubble potion when she noticed a great shadow steal half of the daylight. She looked up and her body crawled in goosebumps. A thick, dark cloud bank rolled across the skies with unnatural speed. A chilled breeze picked up, cutting through the gentle warmth of the day. People pointed to the skies and asked each other questions. Soon the city guards were out as people ran to them for questions.

"Please, remain calm. I'm sure there is a logical explanation for this." The mayor yelled over the growing voices of people speaking their concerns aloud.

An inexplicable blast of icy wind raced through town for a moment. Flags and banners whipped and snapped. Two empty bottles on Tasha's stand blew off and smashed on the stones. The winds died as fast as they had picked up. She bent over to clear up the broken glass when a darker shadow fell over her booth.

"Hello." A Shlan man stood in front of her booth.

Tasha smiled at him. "Oh, uh, hello. Can I help you?"

31

Korvarsk grinned at her, but frowned at the same time. "Perhaps I can help you. You do not look well."

She shook her head. "I feel fine."

"No." He touched her shoulder and repeated, "You don't look well." A shadow flickered across her skin where he made contact, and the veins closest to the surface briefly turned dark black.

Tasha wavered a bit and put a hand to her face. "Oh, what's wrong with me. I...I don't feel well."

"Perhaps you should see a doctor," Korvarsk kindly suggested.

"I will try a potion, I have a few magical healing elixirs left from Donna's old storage."

Korvarsk had a small sneer on his face at the mention of Donna's name, but he quickly pushed it away. "Perhaps that will help," he said. He didn't say anything more, simply walking away and disappearing into the crowd.

Tasha entered the old shop and retrieved a vial of blue potion from a special case. She returned to her stand while sipping the potion, hoping it would alleviate the horrible feeling in her stomach. To her surprise, she saw the same Shlan speaking to another person in the same manner. "What's going on?" She stepped away from her stand, intending to report this man for suspicious behavior to a magistrate, when that sick feeling overwhelmed her. The magistrate and a few others witnessed her fall to the ground, the magic potion bottle shattering against the stones.

The last thing she saw was a group of people around her, with the magistrate looming over her. He gasped and said to the others, "It's the taint..." and then the world went black.

***

"I like it here," Cranshk mused, smiling at a Rakki merchant walking by.

Vulshk, his twin sister, shook her head. "Too many trees. I miss the mountains."

They strolled across the wooden bridges that connected the treehouses of the Rakki capital city. Around them were many Rakki citizens attempting to go about their normal lives in the middle of the national crisis.

A burly Rakki in a guard uniform drew closer to them. Grays tinted his fur, and his sneer was anything but welcoming. He was a beefy man with thick muscles from many hours of intense training.

"What are you two doing out here?" He asked with a brusque tone.

Cranshk answered, "We are guessst of Rema. Under your protection in thisss time of crisis."

The man walked around them, a threatening gaze ever present in his eyes. "Way I heard it, it was the Shlan who are causing a lot of the trouble."

Vulshk said, "That'sss wrong! It wasss a misssssstake." The natural tendency to hiss her words grew worse when she was angry.

The man scoffed, "With Kellus not here and confusing news from Thendor, I don't know what to think. But I think it might be best if you two weren't just wandering the trees." He reached to grab Vulshk by the arm.

Cransk protected his sister by hitting the hand away and then putting himself between them. "I will defend myssself from bulliesss. I am persssonal friends with The Dragon."

"I doubt that." The bully reached for his sword.

"KALVOR!" Shio, Crystal's father, marched out of the healing hut. "What in the Library's name are you doing?"

"My job, Shio."

Shio, displaying no fear, marched closer. "I want to know the reason you would even threaten to pull your sword on a pair of children?"

"They are Shlan." Kalvor stated this as if that was all the evidence he needed.

Shio said, "Since when is that a crime? Have they done anything wrong?"

Kalvor came so close to Shio that his breath was ruffling Shio's fur. "The Shlan attacked the capital. They are not to be trusted!"

Shio slowly shoved his wand into Kalvor's chest, pushing the man back. "We are Rakki of the Blue Forest. We do not threaten children just because they are not Rakki. Now, if you have any legal reason to do what you are doing, tell me. Otherwise, you will find yourself in a very uncomfortable situation quickly."

Kalvor shot both kids a sneer and then a deadly glare at Shio. Without another word, he turned and left.

Taking a moment to calm down, Cranshk finally said, "Thank you."

Shio put his wand away. "I'm sorry about Kalvor. He has always been bitter about Shlan. A long time ago, the last border skirmish took his father's life. That's not an excuse for what he just did."

"We understand. Many Shlan still harbor terrible hatred of your kind. It is wrong."

Shio smiled. "I'm glad to hear you say that. It is certainly wrong." His countenance cheered up as he asked, "Am I right? You two are the Shlan twins. Who are both wizards?"

Vulshk said, "Yes. We are here with other studentsss from the school. They were worried about our safety when that army wasss coming through." She was, of course, referencing the marching of the corrupted Shlan army that attacked Thendor.

"A wise course of action. I have wanted to meet you since Crystal told me about you. I've met no Shlan wizards before."

Cranshk said, "Yesss. There are a few. It isss not common."

Vulshk said, "You are Crystal'sss father."

"I am." He looked over as Fiona left the healing hut. "And that is Crystal's mother."

Fiona walked over while, a perplex expression all over her face. "What's going on out here? You just ran from the hut."

Cranshk said, "He saved usss from a bully."

"Bully?"

Shio said, "Kalvor was pestering them."

"Oh," she answered with complete understanding. "I'm sure he had select words with you two."

"He threatened usss," Vulshk said, a bitter tone in her words.

Fiona shook her head. "Lord Kellus should retire Kalvor. His problem with revenge is not suitable for a peacekeeper."

Rema approached from another direction. "Cranshk, Vulshk, is everything okay?" She looked up at the town's two best medical wizards with a concerned look.

Shio said, "They're fine. Just a problematic encounter. We helped sort it out."

"Oh, good. I'm sure you can tell me all about it at dinner. The innkeeper has prepared a fine meal for all the students." She was gesturing for them to follow.

"Nice to meet you." Cranshk said to Shio.

Vulshk added, "I would love to come and learn some healing charmsss from you."

Fiona said, "I would be my pleasure. Maybe this evening."

They waved to each other before parting.

"I hope you like spicy food. The inn keeper made a large pot of..." Rema paused as the light filtering down through the trees faded quickly. "Bad weather?"

Cranshk shivered. "Something feelsss wrong."

"Look!" Vulshk pointed up at an opening in the trees.

"Is that Markus?" Rema frowned.

They watched a dragon swooping around before turning and leaving quickly.

Cranshk shook his head, "I don't think ssso."

Screaming pierced the air from a distance. Rema pushed the kids behind her and looked back to where they had just been walking from. A woman ran down the wooden path yelling, "TAINT!" Behind the panicking woman lay several people on the path, writhing in pain. Other people were staggering and falling against trees, walls, or the rope railings.

"Oh, dear heavens!" Rema waved at the Shlan. "Move, move, leave! That is no ordinary illness. It is coming toward us quickly."

Shio stumbled out of the healing hut, holding his head and groaning. He was almost a city block away from them, but even at this distance, Rema could see his eyes were wild.

"Shio! Get rid of your wand. Hurry before..."

"PRYMJA!" Shio thrust his wand out and a blast of electricity shot toward them.

Vulshk shouted, "Hlif!" A barrier formed just in time to meet the incoming blast.

Cranshk yelled, "Hrinda!" A force of powerful wind shot toward Shio, and he slammed against the wall of his hut.

The door of the healing hut burst apart under the power of a fire spell. Fiona ran through the smoke, her face even more insane than Shio's.

Rema flipped out her wand and said, "Lami Stor!" A yellow flash exploded, hitting Fiona, Shio and a few others. All fell and were out.

"What did you do to them?" Vulshk asked, a terrified look in her eyes, as though they had fallen dead.

"It is an old paralysis spell. Don't try it yourself. Very tricky. Now, move! Get to the others." Rema turned and ran with them. "Don't let the taint reach more wizards. Run!"

Rema led the students in a mad dash out of the Blue Forest. The taint spread quickly through the trees, with most people falling ill. A few who were able to move helped the others find places to lie.

Running in the fields, the students and teachers from the university moved as fast as the slowest among them.

"Where do we go? Thendor?" One teacher asked.

Rema said, "No. We can't be certain it is safe there yet. We should head for the school. It will be easy for us to protect from the taint there."

Vulshk said, "We have to warn Markus."

"We will." Rema answered, struggling to keep up the pace of these younger, more agile people.

***

Crystal helped Kiin sit up from the bed she had been lying in. "Are you sure you feel fine?"

Kiin stood and stretched. "I'm doing just fine. I don't want to go out and fight a battle right now, but I also don't want to just lay around. There's so much to do. Plus, feeding her is the only time I get to spend with my baby. I want to hold my little girl and do something constructive."

Crystal laughed. "You were always the avid worker. Never sat still long enough for anything, unless it was a task to be completed."

When the door opened, Treb came in, holding their baby girl. "Oh, look, it's Mommy." He was still cooing over the child.

Crystal tattled on Treb to Kiin, "While you want to help out, this man has been nothing but a baby carrier for two days. I don't think I've seen him without the baby since the battle."

"Well, I can help that." Kiin held up her arms, ready for her daughter.

Treb happily placed their child in her arms, and then he stepped closer and smiled at her. "Isn't she beautiful?"

"She is."

Crystal shook her head. "The world is coming apart at the seams, and you two are playing with your baby."

Treb said, "This little girl is my world now."

"I guess that's okay," Crystal answered with a smile.

There was a knock on the door and Donna poked her head into the room. "May I come in?"

"Please," Kiin answered.

Donna walked into the room and paused. "Oh, you're all here. Good." She immediately smiled and swooned. "Oh, isn't that adorable. That baby is just so cute."

"Thanks. I think so too." Kiin answered with a wide grin as she nuzzled the baby's cheek.

Crystal asked, "What did you need to see us about?"

Donna stopped swooning and became deadly serious. "Have any of you talked to Markus recently?"

"I've been in here since the battle," Kiin said.

Treb shook his head. "Now that I think about it, no. I've only seen him in passing, but he's been in his own world. He hardly noticed me."

Crystal agreed with Treb. "I've been busy, but he seems distant whenever I see him too. I figured he has a lot on his mind."

Donna shook her head. "That's the thing. I know Markus. Right now, he has both a family member and his best friend captured by an enemy, and he hasn't said a word about looking for them. This just isn't like him. He would be running around seeking help, gathering information, and forming a plan. When he decided to help the gnomes, he was unstoppable. Now, it seems like he has given up on Korvarsk and Steffen."

Crystal frowned as she said, "You're right. It has been so hectic getting things back together after the battle that I really hadn't had time to think about this. But, he isn't acting normal. Something is wrong."

Treb thoughtfully remarked, "Although he hasn't been physically hurt, he has endured a lot. I mean, he went from being blamed for a massacre to witnessing his best friend betray him and the nation. Then, a relative from the past appears, and things escalate even further. He has been concerned about Kiin, Crystal, You, Steffen, Korvarsk, Gallenor—everything. That's a lot for a seventeen-year-old kid to handle."

Donna paused as she thought about that. "I forget sometimes that he's so young. He acts much older and is so commanding. But, he is just a seventeen-year-old kid."

Crystal added, "Maybe we should stop analyzing him and go help him. He might not be asking for it, but he needs it."

Kiin rocked her baby. "I agree. We..."

"What was that?" Donna turned around suddenly.

Treb frowned. "What? I didn't hear anything?"

"I sense it too," Crystal said as she looked around.

"Come on!" Donna ran out the door with Crystal right behind her.

***

MOMENTS BEFORE:

Markus walked outside the palace, lost in thought. The race lords were still discussing how to handle the Shlan's actions. The guards interrogated Thorne for information and offered Markus a chance to help, but he declined. Instead, he left the palace and quietly walked the streets, deep in thought.

The city was alive with activity but was seasoned with weariness and recovery. It was as if everyone had simultaneously overcome a flu and were just now taking their first shaky steps. However, as in many cases, such widespread disasters often bring out the kindest spirits in everyone.

Markus watched the people rushing around, dealing with the disaster. He didn't think about the damage or the deaths, only about what could come next. "If Steffen is right, then we have to leave Gallenor. Just as the wizards left their lands a thousand years ago, we must leave ours. The corruption will spread. But how can I ask them to leave? Where will we go? How can I abandon my best friend and my great-grandfather?" He talked to himself, hoping that one of those ancient memories would surface to provide all the answers. But nothing came. Continuing to ponder, he said, "It will only cycle again. The corruption will claim Gallenor as it did Kirador and Alanor over a thousand years ago. In time, wherever we move, the darkness will spread. Oh, what do I do!?" He punched a stone wall as hard as he could. "Yeow!" He grabbed his hand and nursed the bruised knuckles. "That was dumb."

"Yes, tell them we'll supply the bread from the palace bakery. The cooks are working on a lot of food." Captain Alex came around a corner and nearly bumped into Markus.

Markus stepped back and nodded to the history's youngest leader of the Royal Guard. "Captain, what are you doing?"

Alex gestured for his subordinates to continue onward. "I'm just helping out, taking care of some of Lord Flavian's recommendations. We have a lot of people to feed and organizing that is no small task."

"What about all the damage caused by the tainted wizards? Aren't your men digging through rubble still?" Markus asked.

"Let me show you something." Alex had a clever smile, as if he had a mighty secret to tell. He led Markus down a street and around a corner. They came to a scene played out many times across the city. People dug through piles of stones and wood to check for survivors and clearing paths. Crawling all over the rubble were Shlan warriors, diligently moving the rubble with speed that was natural to their kind.

Markus' eyebrows were up. "The Shlan army is clearing up the mess?"

Alex nodded. "We had them placed in a camp, as per the recommendation of Lord Flavian, just until the conclusion of the Race Lord conference. They asked to help. They are masters of working around stone and can move across piles of rubble without dislodging anything. So, they won't seriously injure others or themselves by shifting the debris."

Markus nodded. "They are a strange and wonderful people. I hate that the Heart of Darkness used them like this. They had only begun feeling secure after the Morris incident."

Alex smiled. "I will see to it that my men work with them alongside and show friendship. We need to foster that again. One mistake cannot and should not destroy peace between us."

"A good attitude. I'm glad the Captain of the Royal Guard understands these things so well."

Alex said, "Captain Morris understood this as well, a long time ago. He just let his own arrogance and greed take over."

Markus had a voice from his past speaking in his mind. He said, "All it takes is one wrong step to ruin a good person. We have to be careful how we wall, and we always need to be ready to guide misguided friends back when they fall away."

Alex said, "That was very wise."

"Wish I could take credit. I think that's something Tolen once said. But, it is true. The Shlan took a few steps in the wrong direction and led us to what could have been a bloody civil war."

Alex said, "Though a darker power influenced them, I know it only enhanced some ancient mistrust that still sleeps in all our hearts. We all are taught about the animosity that once divided our peoples. Some days, I wish we didn't teach about that and only embraced the friendships. Yet, we should preserve history."

"True, and..." Markus' voice trailed off when he noticed something near the people working around the rubble. "What...what is he doing?"

Alex frowned and looked at the group of Shlan warriors. "Who?"

Markus craned his head to the side as he followed someone with his gaze. "Just a friend. Would you excuse me?"

"Of course. Do you need an escort?"

"No, I'll be fine." Markus left the captain and walked around the corners of the buildings, down the alleys, and right back to the square.

In front of him walked Hlarsk, carrying something. The pudgy old Shlan went to the side of the palace, not facing the square, and set something along a ledge on the wall. He stood back and let out a sigh, seeming to ponder something for a moment.

"What are you doing?" Markus asked quietly.

Hlarsk nearly shed his skin he jumped so hard. "WHAT THE! Oh, it's just you." He stood there, shaking off the surprise. "You move as quietly as a warrior Shlan on the prowl."

Markus shrugged. "I learned how to walk in a special way seven hundred years ago; it's kinda habit now." He looked at what was on the wall and took a step forward. "What is this?"

Hlarsk looked down the line of resting wands, their handles on the ledge, the tips pointing upward. "What little I can do. Everyone is recovering from the taint, my people are helping the royal guard dig out the dead and look for survivors. I'm not strong enough to lift those stones and too fat to walk over them like the younger warriors. So, I'm looking around for lost wands. If I find one, and can touch it, I know the wizard is dead. I bring them back here and have been setting them up like a memorial."

Markus had a sorrowful warm smile, perhaps one of his first genuine smiles since he woke from the dream with Steffen. "That is very kind of you. We're still worried about the living, the memorials haven't really started yet."

Hlarsk gazed at the line of wands. "So many have died. When I look at these, I remember my wife, Korvarsk's mother. A day arrived when my boy returned home to me. I dreamed about it for four years. Finally, the wizards were freed from that damn labyrinth. The evil wizard was vanquished, and Markus the Wise had ushered in a new dawn for Gallenor. At least, that's what everyone else believed. All I

46

saw was my boy, my little, precious boy, coming to his father with tears in his eyes. He handed me my wife's wand and told me she died saving him and so many others. I got my boy back, but I would never see my wife again." Hlarsk spent a moment holding back his sadness.

Markus quietly said, "Too often, people forget the fallen warrior, even while enjoying the peace bought by their sacrifice. I can't forget all those wizards who saved me and Gallenor. Had they not arrived, it would have been a terrible defeat."

Hlarsk gulped hard and said, "I still remember the last day I saw her. She left with our son to obey that stupid decree. They allowed themselves to be trapped in that labyrinth. I hugged her and told her I loved her. She said it wouldn't be long and that they would come back. She held Korvarsk's hand, and they left together with the others. I will never forget that last hug, that final memory of her. It's all I have left to hold onto." He lowered his head. "That and my son. But he's an enemy now. I may never see him again either. I... I can't..." he began to cry, unable to speak.

Markus took Hlarsk in his arms and held him like his own parent who was hurting. "Your son is alive and seeking salvation from this darkness in him."

"Please, Markus, bring my boy back. Please. Don't let him die. I would not want to live a day that he is not alive in this world." Hlarsk was inconsolable.

Markus stood back, holding Hlarsk by the shoulders. "I saw Korvarsk, during the battle."

"You did?" Hlarsk asked with tremulous breaths.

"Yes. Not just his physical self, but I also saw him emerge from the darkness that envelops his mind. He's still inside, trapped within the magic cast by the Dark Heart. I believe he can be liberated. I almost succeeded in freeing him with the purification spell once."

Hlarsk put his head in his hands and wept as he said, "Bring my baby back to me. I don't want to be given his wand."

Markus stood listening to the man sob uncontrollably. It was clear that Hlarsk had held himself together for far too long. Markus could still see Steffen insisting that he not come. He had spent two days forcing himself to numb the reality that Korvarsk and Steffen were gone. He wanted to leave them behind for everyone else's sake. However, that numbness shattered under the weight of Hlarsk's sorrow. He made a decision right then and said, "I will do everything in my power to save him," Markus declared. "This I swear on the honor of my Dragon soul."

Hlarsk looked up, shocked. "On your soul?"

Markus nodded firmly. "I know the Shlan tradition. I swear by the honor of my soul to you, Hlarsk. I will save Korvarsk or die trying."

Still stunned and teary eyed, Hlarsk quietly said, "I accept."

A royal guard came around the palace and stopped in his tracks. "Oh, there you are Lord Dragon. The council wishes your presence and the presence of a man named...Harsk...no, I am so bad at Shlan names."

"Hlarsk?" Hlarsk asked.

"Yes, that's his name."

Markus bowed his head to this young guard, "Thank you. We will be in right away."

"Understood." The guard turned, paused, and then said, "Do you know where the Shlan warrior Hark...Hlarsk is?" He had to focus to make the sound correctly.

Markus nodded. "The mighty warrior, Hlarsk, will be with me. Don't worry."

"Thank you, Lord Dragon." The young man bowed and then rushed away, probably with several more tasks to deal with.

Hlarsk asked, "What do they want with me?"

"I don't know. Here, wipe your eyes." Markus gave Hlarsk a small cloth from his pocket. "Let's go in and find out what this is about."

Hlarsk walked ahead as Markus trailed behind. However, Markus paused when something caught his eye. He knelt, picking up a black wand adorned with a white pearl at the end, examining it closely.

Hlarsk stopped and looked back. "Coming?"

"Yes." Markus continued to examine this particular wand.

Hlarsk and Markus entered the courtroom with over a dozen eyes fixed on them. Markus was the calmer of the two, yet no less curious. Hlarsk looked as though he might faint.

Hlarsk whispered, "That's Lord Kellus and Governor Flavian, I've met them during trade deals before. Oh, and that's Norl the leader of the representatives. And...oh, goodness." He bowed low, "Lord Shashla'yar."

Markus stopped where Hlarsk had suddenly bowed, they were halfway across the room. He spoke loudly, "My Lords, you summoned my friend, Hlarsk, and myself?"

Looking a bit confused, Norl stepped away from the group. "Yes, we did. Please, come forward Master Hlarsk."

Hlarsk gulped and looked up with wide eyes. "Master?"

"What did you say?" Norl frowned at the Shlan language that Hlarsk had just spoken.

Markus whispered, "You have to speak Gallenorian, the translator pendant only works with me and a few others."

"Oh, sorry." He stood and asked, "Why call me a Master?"

Amber of the Momar stepped up. "Aye, I recognized yer name and knew we'd be hav'n a good man to speak to."

"Lady Amber. It isss good to sssee you," Hlarsk said.

Markus had an "ah-ha" look on his face. "That's right. You deal with the Momar in trade relations with the Shlan."

"Aye, he does. An a fine merchant he is if'n I do say so meself. Always a fair dealer, never a silver tongue or a double deal. We can trust inna his testimony."

"Tesstimony?" Hlarsk frowned.

Lord Flavian now spoke, "We have brought you here as a witness to strange events. Your king, Lord Shashla'yar, says your son and this man..." Flavian looked to the side and said, "Bring him in."

Thorne was shoved into the room by a pair of royal guards. "Let go of me! This is expensive fabric!" When Thorne saw Hlarsk, there was a definite surprise in him. "You're alive?"

Flavian continued, "This man, the former Baron Thorne, conspired against your king. The accusation was made that Korvarsk and Thorne were telling lies and manipulating the king to instigate a war. The Lord Dragon has already intimated that your son and Thorne worked for the true enemy, the Dark Heart. Is this true?"

Hlarsk looked at the Baron and then at his king. He hesitated and didn't speak for a long time.

Markus noticed this and whispered, "What is the matter?"

He spoke softly and in Shlan language so that Markus could understand him and the others could not. "I can't implicate my own son. I just can't."

Markus quietly answered him, "Tell them the truth, please. I will protect Korvarsk."

Kellus said, "Please, Master Hlarsk, speak."

51

Hlarsk finally said, "Yesss. I wasss there. My ssson and thisss human plotted and conssspired againssst my people to inssstigate a civil war. A wicked force was controlling them. Pleassse, I know that my ssson isss not himself, he isss not in hisss right mind. Pleassse don't blame him, pleassse." Markus placed a kind hand on Hlarsk's shoulder, to keep him from continuing to beg.

Shashla'yar asked, "Isss it true that Korvarsssk wasss the one who attacked the village in our landsss, not Markusss?"

Hlarsk was on the verge of weeping as he answered meekly, "Yesss. I heard him sssay ssso myself. I know he did thisss to coerce you to blame Markusss. He isss a good boy. Thisss is not my ssson. Believe men. Tell me you believe me."

Everyone looked at each other, Shashla'yar seemed dismayed. Lord Flavian announced, "Then, by this testimony, I move that we end the investigation against King Shashla'yar of the Shlan and accept that he is at no fault of his own, he was acting under misinformation and coercion from outside forces."

Kellus nodded his head to Shashla'yar. "I accept that. The Race Lord conference is concluded, the blame will rest with Korvarsk and former Baron Throne."

"Please, do not blame my son, please." Hlarsk was now begging again in his own tongue.

Markus summoned his Dragonwand and held it before him, a sign that he wished to speak as the Dragon and wanted the court's attention. Everyone became silent and looked at him with a bit of confused shock. He declared, "The blame is not with Korvarsk, but that which is controlling him. During the purification, Korvarsk was freed long enough for me to sense the real man under the darkness. He is being controlled and held back, his actions are not his own. However, I do not sense the same dual personality in Thorne; I don't even sense the darkness in him. The only darkness in him was bred in his own soul. The blame rests with him and with the Dark Heart in the matter of coercion and corruption of the Shlan king and court."

Lord Kellus said, "I'm sorry, Lord Dragon, but you do not have the say on this matter. The final decision on these matters rests with the court. This court will decide who is accused of what crime."

Markus smiled. "I refuse to hurt my friend. I promised to do everything I could to save him, but I will not kill Korvarsk. None among you possess that power or authority. While you may seek to blame him, I will not. In matters concerning Dragons, I hold the authority; I am the bearer of the first Dragonwand, heir to the leader's seat on the Dragon Council, and a descendant of Tolen the Wise and Steffen, the first Dragon. Is this understood?"

Lord Kellus was stunned and a bit upset with Markus for the first time. "Yes, it is understood."

"I do not mean to undermine this court, but I will do so only when absolutely necessary. But, on this matter, I shall not change my mind."

Lord Flavian answered, "We will respect your authority to a point, Lord Dragon. But, you must understand that the safety of Gallenor is our responsibility."

"I know. I will find a way to free Korvarsk and defeat this enemy. I will bring security back to Gallenor by ending the threat of..." Markus wavered and held his head, his Dragonwand vanished from his hand as he stumbled into Hlarsk.

Hlarsk held him up. "What is the matter? Are you okay?"

Markus groaned and fought to stay up. "Something is wrong... terribly wrong."

Just then, the windows around the palace grew darker, blocking the sunlight that filtered through. The open doors of the court also became dark, and voices could be heard outside screaming in panic.

A man ran up the steps and came into the court. "A strange storm is hovering over the city. The clouds aren't natural."

The people of the court rushed to see what was happening, everyone except Markus. He stood there, clutching Steffen's wand in his hands while Hlarsk supported him. Markus struggled as he said, "I...I can feel him. The pain...it's so intense. What is happening?" He collapsed and passed out, still gripping the wand in his hands, the Pearl on top glowing brightly.

"Markus!" Hlarsk shook his shoulder, hoping to wake him.

Just then a darker shadow flew over the area, followed by screams. People dashed away from the square with one word on their lips, "Dragon!"

"What's going on!" Donna came running in with Crystal right beside her.

"Markus!" Crystal was at his side quickly, checking him over and assessing his condition. "What happened to him? Why is he down?"

"I don't know. He just passed out after those clouds came over." Hlarsk was so scared that his tail trembled.

Donna peered at the wand in Markus' hands. "Where did he get that? Why is it glowing?"

Crystal held her wand over Markus. "I can't say, but he isn't injured. It's like he's asleep."

A voice called out from the square. "MARKUS!"

Hlarsk was the first to look back at the door. In a dry voice he said, "Korvarsk."

"Markus! Come out here at once!"

Hlarsk slowly got back up and made his way to the door.

Crystal said, "You can't go, he'll kill you."

Hlarsk firmly said, "I'd rather die than hide from my own son." Without another word, he walked outside.

CHAPTER 3: REUNION

KORVARSK, now a Shlan, was surrounded by a legion of royal guards, accompanied by twice as many Shlan and a few wizards. They all maintained a safe distance, yet were ready to strike at a moment's notice. Despite the threatening crowd around him, Korvarsk showed no fear. The look in his eyes radiated pure wickedness when he said, "Father, how surprising. You should be dead."

"I survived to save you and all of Gallenor. Please, stand down. Let us help you."

Korvarsk glared at his father with narrowed eyes. "I don't need help; I only need to complete my task."

Hlarsk walked down the steps of the palace. "Korvarsk, please, don't do this. Come with me, we can find a way to help you."

Korvarsk smiled, slithering his tongue menacingly at his father. "I am perfectly fine."

"Don't you slither at me! Respect your father and stand down now!"

Korvarsk strolled toward the steps, continually watching Hlarsk. The guards and wizards remained vigilant but hadn't attacked yet. "Oh, I need your help right now," he said, holding up his hand.

Hlarsk reached out, eager to grip his son's hand again. When their palms met a sick darkness seeped out from Korvarsk and poured over their hands. However, Korvarsk screamed and lurched back, holding his wrist. "WHAT IS THIS!?"

Hlarsk, confused and dismayed, looked at his hand. "I don't know what happened."

Korvarsk hissed loudly and glanced at the people. "Purified, purified, all of you. The damned light is still protecting you! Damn Steffen and his foolish plan!" He paused for a moment, hearing the guards' footsteps slowly approaching around him. "So confident now that I am unable to taint you. But you quickly forget what I can do. If I can't taint this city, I will wipe it out!" He reached out, and his Dragonwand materialized in his hand. Everyone present recoiled at the sight of the powerful wand. The guards jumped between citizens and Korvarsk.

From within the palace came a bright blast of magic. It hit Korvarsk in the chest, sending him flying backward across the ground, his wand tumbling free and vanishing.

Donna stood on the top steps of the palace, her Dragonwand held out from where she had just stopped him. "Not today! I have already learned much from this wand, and you never truly defeated me in combat."

Korvarsk hissed, "Foolish, pathetic woman! You haven't fought me. I will destroy you."

Donna returned his fury with a confident resolve. "You and I both know that within me is the memory and skill of the master who held this before. The only dragon that the dark heart fought and never defeated."

"You know nothing, Chais!" Korvarsk screamed.

Donna held up her wand with one hand and pulled out a potion vial with her other. "I'm not Chais, I just have his memories. I'm Donna, potion master and Dragon. I'll tear your tail off and feed it to you. You corrupted my mind, I haven't forgotten that. You threaten my kingdom, I will defend that. And, you took my man, I will not forgive that. However much you fear Chais, fear Donna much, much more." She casually walked down the steps.

Korvarsk summoned his wand again. "So arrogant. What potion can hurt me?"

Donna tossed the bottle up and down with her hand. "I may not have Steffen's purifying light, but I remember one thing about fighting darkness: all light hurts." She threw the bottle, and it shattered, spreading the liquid across the middle of the square. The liquid emitted a bright white glow that was hard to look at for any normal person, but for Korvarsk, it was downright painful.

He raised his arms, attempting to shield himself from the light. "This is not over! It has only begun. She will possess the core soon, and then your arrogance will be repaid!" In a swift motion, Korvarsk transformed into a dragon and soared into the sky, darting away from the light and out of the city.

Donna watched him leave and told Captain Alex, "Make sure to keep watch. If he gets close at all, call Markus or me. We can't let him attack this city. He'll bring terrible destruction like the attack on the Port of Pearls."

"Yes, Lady Dragon," Alex responded, quickly running to the Royal Guard and Shlan warriors.

Donna turned around, ready to head back inside and see what was wrong with Markus. Her path was blocked by a man on his knees weeping. Two others were beside him, consoling him as best they could. Hlarsk's body shook and his sobs deep. Kneeling, she put a hand on Hlarsk's shoulder and said, "It's okay. He's gone. You're fine."

"No, I'm not. My son is gone. I held his hand...I..." he was lost in sorrow.

"Come on, we need to get back inside." She helped him up and led him inside the palace.

***

Markus was on his knees in that dark realm again. He still gripped Steffen's wand tightly, which seemed strange since he wasn't in the real world, and he knew it. Cautiously rising to his feet, he glanced around. "Steffen?"

"Steffen is not here," a gentle female voice answered.

Markus frowned. "Who's there?"

"Please, you have to come to me." That voice was soft and kind.

Markus saw a distant light and walked toward it. He quickly covered the distance, though his stride never broke a simple stroll. In a matter of seconds, he was in a room he recognized. It was his bedroom back in his home in the Valley. This was surprising, but Markus hardly noticed the room for the person seated on a pillow in the corner. This was not a pillow he had ever seen, though he did recognize the person. This was the form the Dark Lady took of Steffen's late wife, with dark fur, a long tail, and a feline face and ears.

Taking a step back, he tried to summon his Dragonwand, but it did not come, so he pointed Steffen's wand at her. "You! How did you get me in here?"

Alieth smiled at him with no fear in her eyes. Her gentle voice asked, "I have always been here. Where is this place?" Looking around, she seemed amused by the stuff in his room.

Markus did not lower his defenses. "If you've always been here, why ask about this place?"

She picked up a small stuffed bear and brushed her hand over its head. "I'm part of Steffen's wand, I'm in the Pearl. This place is yours. When you approached me, the most comfortable memory from your past came to you and created this place. You must have felt very safe and content in this room."

"I don't believe you. You're the demon witch who has stolen my friend and tainted this world."

She set the bear down and became sad. "I'm sorry for what the Dark Pearl has done, but I'm not a part of that. I'm the last shard of memory that Steffen won't let go of. I'm the source of his light in the wand he carries."

Markus slowly lowered the wand. "You're part of the wand? Then am I in..."

"Yes, you are in the wand, your mind at least. The light magic in your soul connected with this wand in a time when a terrible darkness must have surrounded you."

It all came back to his mind. "The sky outside went dark. I felt a horrible pain in my chest and then... I don't remember."

"A darkness spread around you. The darkness of the wicked pearl was attempting to overcome your mind. It would never succeed, the light in you is far too strong for that. But, the attack was still dangerous. Through the shared light in here and in you, I was able to bring your mind in here and protect you from the pain."

"Are you a spell or are you his late wife?"

"Neither. I am just a memory of Steffen's. The real Alieth died almost three thousand years ago. You see, Steffen could never let her go. He tore this last shard of memory out of his mind and placed it in the wand he carried. He can focus his light magic and do great things with this memory here. But, only because he had the light in him as well. It is no longer in him, not as it was before."

"What do you mean?"

"Somehow, his light has dimmed and shifted. He remains strong and still wields a powerful light, but it's nothing compared to what he had before. It's nothing compared to what I'm feeling in you right now."

"In me?"

"Yes. Do you not sense it? Do you not see it? The light magic in you is as powerful as Steffen once was."

"After the purification spell I cast, I began to wonder. I honestly didn't want to believe it." Markus sat on the edge of his old bed. "That is what he was talking about. He said that the light is in me. For some reason, the Dark Lady needs this light and captured him instead of me. He wants me to leave Gallenor so she cannot get me. But, how could he lose the light? He is untouchable by the taint."

Alieth reached over and placed a hand on his knee. "He lost the light due to immeasurable guilt. He blames himself for the suffering caused by the darkness. He failed to stop her before and now faces her again. He created her when he attempted to take his own life. I suspect he wants her to kill him."

"Why would he want that?" Markus asked.

"I am just a memory; I don't understand why he would do this. However, I suspect he wishes to die now for the same reason he tried to die three thousand years ago."

Markus glanced at Alieth, and a cold realization washed over him. "He didn't want to live without you. He hasn't let go of you all these years. This memory in here, that corrupted memory out there—it's all part of his inability to move on."

Alieth smiled. "Yes and no. He holds dearly to me, but his heart did change one day. He opened it briefly and let someone else in. I suppose you know who that was."

Markus frowned and thought about that, "Donna...he was flirting around with her. No, that..." Looking up he remembered the last thing Steffen said, "Tolen. His son."

"Yes. For centuries after the real Alieth's death, he had a cold heart; although kind and good, he didn't allow anyone to bring him the joy he believed he had lost. Then, he found his son and raised him, which gave him a reason to live."

Markus looked down at the wand in his hands. "He loved his son as any father should. But, Tolen was ashamed of how Steffen failed to kill the Dark Lady. Tolen had to finish the last Dragon war by sacrificing himself while Steffen sat in the Sea Fairy kingdom. He never got to say goodbye to Tolen. Is this what has removed the light from Steffen?"

"No, his light was not removed because of any darkness in him, but because of the love in him. He thought he lost Tolen, but found Tolen again." She held her hand out as a black cloth appeared on the bed beside Markus.

Markus lifted the cloth and discovered it was the cloak Steffen had given him. "Tolen's cloak. Steffen gave this to me on the mountainside. I thought he was just being nice, but I guess he was giving it back."

"Correct. He sees in you the boy he raised and loved dearly. You are the son he thought he would never see again. Yes, Tolen is gone, but never lost while you are here. You hold his wand, you have his wisdom, and you even look a little like him when he was your age."

"But, I'm not Tolen. Tolen was my great, great... really great grandfather from long ago."

She laughed. "Time doesn't matter, you are that which he wanted for his son... greatness. You show compassion and joy, you show love and wisdom. Without the wand, you had these. Tolen's wisdom and memories didn't give you what wasn't already there. They only enhance it. You bright hope to Steffen's life that his son lived, loved, and was happy. You have given Steffen the same hope and joy that he once found when he discovered Tolen's soul had survived."

Markus asked, "How do I save Steffen?"

"I don't know. As I said, I am just a shard of a memory. I have seen what Steffen sees for a long time but do not have the answers. I can say that I am tied to him just as the dark memory is tied to him out there. Both that wicked demon and I are part of him and he knows it. This is why he feels guilty. He feels he must sacrifice himself to protect you and this world from his past. You must save him or he will surely die and the darkness will not stop seeking power until you too are gone."

"That doesn't make sense? I don't understand."

"I wish I had more answers. However, I do not. For you, it is time to wake up...wake up..."

Crystal's voice took over Alieth's and kept repeating, "Wake up... wake up..."

He opened his eyes and saw that he was still on the ground in the courtroom, with Crystal casting an enchantment over him. "What's happening?" he asked as he attempted to sit up.

She stopped and smiled. "Oh, good. I couldn't get any spell to work. You were completely lost."

"No. I wasn't lost, just deep in thought." He looked up at the windows. "What's going on? Where did these clouds come from? It was such a sunny day."

Donna stood beside him, still holding her Dragonwand, "I'm afraid things have gotten a lot worse."

***

The Dark Lady sat on her throne, watching the life drain from Steffen and fill her Dragonwand core. Still in the form of Alieth, she gleefully smiled at her victim hanging in the air before her. Her most loyal companion, Kellen, never left her side, always clutching the Pearl in silence. Steffen had stopped reacting to the pain hours earlier and now just hung, suspended in the air by magical chains. The only real sounds came from outside, where the assorted noises of dark creatures rumbled throughout the wastelands. Occasionally, a terrifically deep thump would boom as one of her behemoth creations moved about.

"Is he dead yet?" Kellen ventured a question, watching the limp body strung up in the room by the chains.

She answered, "No. If he were to die, then I could no longer drain the magic from him. His life remains intact."

"Does he not need to eat? If you need him to remain alive for this to work, he should need food."

The Dark Lady stood and walked casually toward Steffen. "His body is remarkable. He can survive a long time without food or water. It is his curse and his blessing, immortality." She came closer to the Dragonwand core floating before Steffen.

Steffen lifted his head, a weakness in his eyes as his magic was drained. He sternly whispered, "Take off that face."

She smiled and ran her hand over her furry face. "Oh, but it is my true face. Don't you remember? You created me; I am this person."

"You are not Alieth. You are a cursed creation, a mere shadow of life. You will never know half of the true strength that Alieth had."

She chortled at him. "So brave, so strong. If only you had accepted my offer all those centuries ago and become my king. We could rule this world in darkness."

"You will never rule this world. You have already failed and don't even realize it." He slumped over, unable to maintain this facade of brave strength.

Turning, she once again gazed at the core. "I will have all that I want, in due time. I..." She touched the core and lost her smile. "What is this?"

Kellen stood quickly and hesitantly asked, "Is something wrong, my lady?"

"The core is not growing as I expected. Something is not right here."

"What? Can I help?" Kellen asked eagerly.

"Be silent!" She boomed, which sent Kellen hunkering down in fear.

Steffen laughed, his head still hung low as he no longer had strength to hold it up. "You've been so focused on me that you missed it. You planned this for centuries but made one fatal mistake."

She turned back to him and snapped her fingers. An invisible force pulled his head up to look at her. "Whatever little games you're trying to play will not work. I'm superior to you, always have been."

Just then, a heavy flapping of wings grew loud as something approached. Korvarsk came through one of the huge windows and nearly crashed into the ground. Instantly, he was a Shlan again. He grimaced and held his right hand with his left.

"Show me!" The Dark Lady demanded.

He revealed his hand, the palm still marred by streaks of burned scaly skin. "I failed."

"What is this? What are you doing back so soon?" she asked.

Korvarsk huffed as he walked by her. "I was able to taint most of Gallenor."

"Most?" She was furious.

"The college was protected by a barrier I could not get through easily."

"The college? But it was vacant when we passed that with the Shlan armies."

"It isn't now. Also, Thendor remains purified. I was injured when I touched one of them." He neglected to mention it was his father, a man she had ordered him to kill long before now.

Turning to Steffen, her smile returned. "So, this is your little ploy. Try to cut off some of the taint in hopes it will weaken me?" Steffen was laughing, his head still held up. She cut her hand to the side and his head flopped back down. Turning sharply to Korvarsk she asked, "Has the darkness spread in the skies?"

"Should be across every province by now."

Calmer, the lady walked back toward her throne. "Then, my plans will suffice. Two little locations will hardly impact my power. Eventually, they too shall fall."

Korvarsk said, "If you return with me to the college, I'm sure we can break through their barrier. Markus and Donna will fight me if I go back alone, and I won't be able to take them on alone."

Sitting with a regal posture, she answered, "No. Your work is done for now. In a short time, the core will be complete and my reign of death and destruction will begin."

Kellen quietly asked, "My lady, when will I gain more power? I too wish to be a Dragon? Surely, there are other cores. If we find one, perhaps you can also corrupt it for me."

With a dismissive laugh she waved a hand at him. "I shall never allow you to hold the Pearl and a core. I will not allow you to become a Dragon. I did that once and was betrayed. You will remain the custodian of the Pearl and that position will be sufficient."

"Yes…my lady," Kellen whispered, defeated.

***

Captain Alex came into the courtroom and approached the gathered leadership. Markus stood to the side, quietly watching as the others diligently worked. Captain Alex knelt before Lord Norl and Lord Flavian, both at the front of the room.

Flavian spoke to the captain, "Report, please."

"We have placed wizards and guards along the wall. So far, no sign of the Dragon. The wizards have cast a barrier spell that should ward off unwanted dark creatures."

Lord Flavian bowed his head. "Good work. Please, keep us posted hourly unless there is significant change."

"Yes, my lord." Captain Alex bowed his head, stood, and left.

Norl held up a parchment. "We've had reports from the Port of Pearls, Momar Land, Shlan land, and Stillwater. All are experiencing a quick outbreak of the taint."

Lord Kellus hesitantly asked, "Have we heard from the Blue Forests?"

Norl shook his head, "Not yet. We sent a courier to the forests, but it will take time."

Shashla'yar added, "I sssent one of my best and quickest, she will return sssoon with information."

Flavian smiled at Shashla'yar. "Thank you. Your people have been invaluable in this, their legendary quickness has proven useful."

Amber stepped up. "Lord Dragon. What have you to say on this?"

Deep in thought, Markus looked up and spent a moment gathering the words. "It is as I feared. She is spreading taint to gain power. Steffen told us that the taint gives her strength. With almost all of Gallenor infected, she will grow beyond anything we can do."

"Is this to weaken us?" Amber asked.

Markus stated, "The situation is complicated. Yes, it will weaken us. When she implements her ultimate plan, we will be broken and powerless against her. But it is this sickness, this taint, that she draws power from."

Flavian said, "I have never truly understood how that works."

"I can't say that I understand it," Markus admitted.

Amber asked, "How can the Lord Dragon, who is full o the memory of all his ancestors, not understand such a thing?"

Markus said, "It is the fool who believes that he knows it all. You find wisdom when you admit what you don't know. In this case, the taint, this deep darkness, is the opposite of the power that fuels my most powerful magic. It is difficult for me to understand simply because I am so opposed to its very existence. A fish might see a bird fly and even understand that water and air are different, but the concept of flight will still confuse it, no matter how well explained."

Flavian asked, "What did you mean that this gives her power? Do you understand that?"

"In a way. I don't know how it works, precisely. But I know that this taint is just a symptom of the power that fuels the darkness in her. The more taint in this world, the further and stronger the power of her taint is. It is as a sickness that feeds on a person. It makes them ill. The more sick they are, the more of the illness is in them. As they are on their deathbed, the more of the plague is in their body. But, just as a dead body no longer gives the illness a place to thrive, once all life extinguishes in this land from the taint, the darkness will grow weak again. It consumes life, but in a diametrically opposing idea, it needs life to exist."

"So, we find a cure, and keep it from spreading?"

Marku said, "We can't cure people fast enough. The only way to stop this from killing thousands of citizens, and ultimately rendering this land as barren as the northern wastes, is to destroy the source of the taint."

"Then, we must act now!" Kellus demanded.

Markus paced with a furrowed brow. "We need a plan of attack, a strategy. But I don't know what to do. I've been considering what I learned from Steffen's wand and sorting through all my memories from Tolen. I just can't figure this out. I can't think of a way to deal with her, and we can't afford to fail."

Since Markus could understand, Lord Shashla'yar said in his tongue, "What about the purification spell you used. It worked on us and cleansed everyone quickly. We could cleanse the other lands."

Markus shook his head. "It would take time, which we are running out of. She has a Dragonwand core and means to use it. I

72

know she cannot fully access it, but she can still garner a lot of power through it. The taint is only part of her strength. No, we must defeat this at its source. I just don't know how."

Kellus asked, "What about purifying her? You could cast that spell and cleared this whole town in seconds. Surely, just one person would be unable to resist purification."

"No, I thought about that too," Markus said. "Korvarsk was closer to me than most of those who were tainted. He suffered a brutal impact from the light magic. It rattled the darkness within him, but she quickly regained control. Plus, she was only using him. I don't believe she can be cleansed like the taint."

Amber quietly said, "Then we're dead."

Markus pulled out Steffen's wand. "Not yet. There is an answer to this problem, I know it. I just have to figure it out. I have over a thousand years of memories in my head, and there has to be an answer buried somewhere."

Crystal ran into the room with Donna beside her. "The Blue Forests are tainted!"

Everyone stopped and looked at her with curious eyes. Lord Kellus asked, "What was that?"

She stopped and held up a letter. "I just received a magic letter from Vulshk. She said that the Blue Forests have been tainted. People started coming down with the taint."

Markus quickly asked, "Where are the wizard students?"

Donna replied, "Rema had all the students escorted out of the woods as soon as the taint appeared. She knows well how the taint affects wizards."

"Then, where are they?" Kellus asked.

"Rema guided them back to the college. They cast a barrier charm over the school to protect it from the taint. They spotted a dragon flying overhead, but it did not stop to attack. Instead, it flew north."

Amber asked, "Why north? The Shlan lands are already tainted."

Markus answered, "He is not heading for the Shlan lands, he is heading to where the Dark Lady is preparing the core and creating her dark army."

"How do you know this?" Flavian asked.

"The wastelands have been tainted before. The darkness in the far north has been a plague on this land since its founding. The ship she was trapped in is now a haven for dark magic. I have no doubt she is building her forces up there. That is where we will have to confront her. I just don't know how."

"Then, we must prepare ourselves," Flavian stated.

Markus asked, "How? I don't even know how to defeat her."

Kellus replied, "We will invade that land whether or not you devise a magical solution. We will not sit back and let this nation succumb to the taint."

Shashla'yar proudly declared, "All my forcesss will march with the ressst of Gallenor."

Kellus said, "The Rakki archers will fight as well."

Flavian said, "I will summon any support from the Port of Pearls."

Crystal whispered to Markus, "Why are you smiling? This is not really a time for happiness."

"It is, actually." He spoke loudly to everyone, "Please, by all means, plan for battle, prepare strategy. But, let me think about this. If we want to win this, we need more than brute force."

The lords nodded in respect to him and began to speak to one another about troop arrangements and tactics. The Shlan king took lead, as he was more experienced in troop arrangement and also how to traverse the mountains.

"I'll help," Donna approached the Lords.

Lord Kellus kindly said, "Lady Dragon, we respect your title, but you are a potion master and teacher, I doubt tactics are your strength."

"Maybe not just yet. But I hold the memories of Chais, the last Dragon of Earth. He was a tactical genius, earning that reputation while battling the forces of darkness. He was the only Dragon to confront the Dark Dragon of Hallond without ever losing or being tainted. I believe I can contribute some ideas to your planning."

"Sounds like a good idea." Flavian waved her over to the group.

Crystal followed Markus as he walked toward the doors to the square. "What should I do to prepare?" She asked, a boldness in her posture and tone.

Markus took her hand. "Nothing. You aren't going into battle."

"I most certainly am going."

He kissed her hand and shook his head. "I cannot allow that. Please, just go and make sure that those still healing get the best treatment from the finest medical wizard in all of Gallenor."

She grunted and huffed. "Why do you have to be so charming when you are being so mean to me?"

"Not mean, just protective." He kissed the back of her hand and left to step outside.

CHAPTER 4: FAMILY

THE long, black wand rolled between his fingers as Markus looked at the large white pearl secured to the top. Citizens watched in curiosity as he paced around the Central Square in front of the palace. The massive doors were open, as was tradition, and this let him hear the constant planning among the Shlan, Rakki, and human leaders. He easily overheard her opinions on their current strategy. He wished he could go in and give them an answer, something precise to work off of to make this battle work. Tolen was no war general. He didn't have answers for this kind of talk.

"There has to be something in my memories. A clue, a weakness, something." He fumed to himself. Since he became the Lord Dragon, he has relied on these ancient memories to guide him. People looked up to him. The leaders of this land have gladly accepted his wisdom and sought it often. Now, in their darkest time, his wisdom felt empty.

A woman rolled a wagon filled with fruit across the cobblestone street. Markus watched her. She would stop and hand people a bit of fruit before moving on. The skies remained covered in strange, boiling, ominous clouds. The protection barrier around the city flickered now and then, reminding everyone it was still there. To say that there was tension in the air would be an understatement. The people had hope, but it was seasoned with a healthy amount of fear.

An elderly man cautiously walked up to Markus and bowed as best as he could. "My Lord Dragon."

"Don't bow so low, sir. I wouldn't want you to hurt your back."

"How kind of you to think of me." He straightened up. "I have heard the race generals in there speaking of war. Are we going to be under attack again?"

The palpable fear in him hurt Markus's heart. The Dark Lady loved to spread this kind of dire panic. "Not here. But we will face our enemy on the battlefield soon. We will bring the fight to them. Don't worry."

"Oh, so we will take them on? Will you fight them?"

Markus frowned. "I will certainly defend this land."

A smile brightened the wrinkled face. "Then we have great hope. The Lord Dragon will defeat any enemy." He walked away happier than when he approached.

Markus liked that this brought joy to him, but he felt a pressure like never before. He had to find an answer. The nation was in his hands. This idea drew his eyes back on the wand and his confusing problem.

"I just don't understand. What do I do? That Dark Lady is tied to Steffen, and so is the piece of Alieth memory in this wand. How can I use this to free Korvarsk and Steffen? How do I end this?" As he repeated this over and over, he only became more angry; it was not generating any answers. In a petulant outburst, he screamed, "Why don't I have the answer?"

A calm voice said, "You don't have to have all the answers. Sometimes, just doing what you can is all that is needed."

Hlarsk walked down the steps from the palace holding Treb and Kiin's baby in his arms. He sat down while saying, "I do know that screaming and fussing is about the worst way to figure out a problem." The Shlan gently rocked back and forth, smiling at the tiny white Rakki infant.

"Hlarsk. What are you doing?" Markus approached with a frown on his face.

Hlarsk continued to gaze at the little girl. "That nice Rakki woman needed someone to hold her baby while she changed into her armor. The old woman who has been looking after this one is currently asleep. I have some experience with babies, so I volunteered."

"That was nice of you." Markus sat next to Hlarsk.

"It wasn't entirely selfless, I needed to feel like I was doing something helpful. Also, I want to remember that time when life made sense. I remember holding my little hatchling, watching him sleep, his mother roasting a nice beetle for dinner. I never imagined a day without her or him. But, now I've lost both of them."

"You haven't lost Korvarsk," Markus stated firmly.

Kiin came through the doors, decked out in her standard Rakki armor. "Okay, thanks. I'll take her back now." She held out her arms, ready for her little girl.

Hlarsk gently handed the precious bundle up to Kiin. "There you go. She just nodded off."

Markus asked, "Why are you getting ready for combat? You just recovered from one battle and had a baby. You're in no shape to fight."

"I have to go. I was once the Captain of the Blade Warriors. Captain Rulth was injured during the fight here and can't stand. I have to lead the Blade Warriors into this battle. Besides, I have to protect Gallenor for my baby."

Markus nodded as he said, "I understand. I just wish it hadn't come to this."

"I don't want to do this, but I have to. I think it's time to put this one down for a full nap." Kiin returned to the palace.

Markus, sitting beside Hlarsk, gazed up at the sky. The peculiar appearance of the clouds made his stomach flutter every time. "What should I do?" he whispered.

Hlarsk quietly said, "Markus, I need to tell you something."

"What is it?"

"I am absolving you of your duty to me. Your soul oath to me is undone."

Markus gave Hlarsk a curious glance. "What? I'm not giving up on this. Just because I don't have the answer yet doesn't mean I've quit."

"I know, and I know that you'll still try. But, I don't want you to neglect Gallenor for the sake of one Shlan. Korvarsk is now a tool of the enemy, a danger to this world. If it comes down to it, you must kill him."

"You can't possibly mean that! How can you say that with such ease?"

Hlarsk slowly lowered his head. "I can say this because of what I'm about to ask you."

"What?"

"Markus...would you end my life?"

Markus leaned away, his eyes wide and his mouth hung open. "You...you want me to kill you?"

"Yes. Not now, but I don't want to know if you have to kill Korvarsk to save this world. I don't want to be handed his wand like his mother's, I don't want to live knowing my son's body lies in a wasteland, having been defiled by evil magic. I want you to come back and take my life without telling me he is dead."

Markus was speechless for a moment; he sat there, unable to process this. Finally, he softly answered, "I can't do that. It would be murder. Even with your consent, I would never forgive myself for it."

Hlarsk had not lifted his head and remained that way as he explained. "Just after I learned of my wife's death, I became angry and mean. I longed for her and felt bitter. I even hated you, long before I knew you, of course. I hated the whole world. I didn't want to go on without her. I loved her so much. But I looked up from my pain and saw the eyes of another person who was in just as much pain—my son. Not only had he lost his mother, but his father had become a monster. I said things to him that I would never have said. When I realized I still had him, I was able to let her go. I still have her in my heart and think about her often, but life goes on. Without Korvarsk, I don't have anyone to turn to, anyone to hold on to. My world will be destroyed."

"I know you feel like you will not have anyone left, but that isn't true. You have friends."

Hlarsk put a hand on Markus's shoulder and said, "I treasure our friendship and those I have made among many people. Few Shlan have as many non-Shlan friends as I. But... they aren't my family. Nothing can replace my son."

"You let go of your wife. If Korvarsk falls, you can let him go." Markus dug for any way he could save Hlarsk from asking this.

Hlarsk buried his face in his hands. "How can I let go of him? It tore me apart to let her go, but to let go of my son as well? I just can't. I don't want to. I'd rather die than face that."

Markus scooted over a few inches and wrapped his arm around Hlarsk's back. "You'll have me. Korvask has become like family, which means you're family too. I won't let you face this world alone. I promise. Darkness is not the answer, look for the light, in spite of pain. Don't let the bitterness of loss drive you..." Markus began to realize something.

Hlarsk leaned over against Markus. "It's just...I held his hand, I looked him in the eye. It was not my son looking back at me."

Markus sat up straight and lifted Hlarsk's face. "Your son is in there, I know it. And I think I finally understand how to free him."

"You do?" Hlarsk wiped his eyes.

Markus laughed with glee. "You provided me with the answer."

Hlarsk was perplexed. "What? How?"

Standing, Markus felt a surge of excitement and happiness. "The darkness thrives on darkness. It feeds on all the negativity in this world. The Dark Lady was created from a moment of profound darkness within the man who is the source of light. That was an incredibly powerful darkness, and its thread still lingers. It must be severed, and he is the one to do it. It all makes sense now. She exists because he won't let her go. She exists because of him. Oh, this makes perfect sense... it finally makes sense."

Hlarsk was scared of Markus. "I have no idea what you're saying."

Markus leaned over and took Hlarsk by the shoulders. "I'm saying that I know how to free Korvarsk, and that is all you need to understand. You will get your son back, I promise. I'm not letting you forgive my oath, I am still holding to it. I swear on my heart, soul, and honor that Korvarsk can be freed and I will do it. Now, I have to go join a planning meeting." He rushed back inside, leaving poor Hlarsk confused but more hopeful than he was a moment ago.

A large table had been brought into the courtroom, and on it was a map of the lands in and around Gallenor. Lord Shashla'yar provided them with the exact location of the ancient shipwreck his people had guarded for centuries.

Flavian, Kellus, Shashla'yar, and Donna stood around the table, with Captain Alex nearby. Tension was in the air as they all looked at the map and spoke to one another.

"Are you sure this is the location?" Flavian asked.

Shashla'yar nodded. "One of the lassst scout reportsss I read before leaving to invade Thendor sssaid that a lot of dark creatures were amasssing near the wreck."

Donna added, "Markus and Steffen both faced her near that wreck in the ancient lost wizard city. It makes perfect sense."

"Then, that will be our destination." Kellus looked up at Donna. "Lady Dragon, are you sure you will have enough time?"

Donna nodded. "Yes. With help from the local potionsmiths, I can have enough brewed in around a day; it isn't that complicated of a potion."

"Good. Get started as soon as you can," Kellus said. "We need every ounce of help we can get in a battle like this."

Flavian asked, "How do you know what kind of forces we will face up there? We don't even know if she is gathering forces. Should we wait until our scouts can bring us information?"

Donna answered, "Markus told us what he and Steffen faced when they were there looking for his lost wand. At that point, she hadn't even started sparking the war between the Shlan and Thendor, and she already had impressive forces. I doubt she will neglect to grow her numbers."

Markus entered. "Donna is right. We must presume that significant forces are poised to confront us. One truth I have learned over the eons of memories is that power breeds paranoia. The Dark Lady continues to gain strength, growing her power, and waiting for the Dragonwand core to belong to her. Until she possesses ultimate power, she will feel paranoid that someone might come along and seize it. Worse still, she has attempted this twice before and failed, which will only ignite the flames of paranoia in her heart. She will have an army ready for us... in fact, she will unleash monsters of darkness unlike anything Gallenor has ever witnessed."

Flavian solemnly said, "Markus, I hope you come with good news and not just grim wisdom."

Markus approached the table and slowly met their eyes. He gave off a smile and set Steffen's wand down before them. "I have a plan."

Shashla'yar asked, "Well...what is it?"

"All this time, I've been trying to figure out how to destroy her, to use the light within me like Steffen did to cure the taint. But now I realize it's not just about me; it's about him. I need to return this wand to Steffen. He doesn't understand—or rather, he fails to admit—that the power to end the Dark Lady forever has always been within him. I have to get him this wand and convince him of what he must do."

Kellus frowned. "How can a wand stop her? He had it before and she wasn't stopped."

Markus slowly picked up the wand again. "Steffen didn't fully understand what he had to do." There was a pause as Markus considered how to say this. Finally, he said, "It is far too complicated to explain; you just have to trust me."

Flavian said, "We trust you, Markus the Wise. However, there is no second battle here. If we fail, then Gallenor falls, as does the world. Please, we need to know more."

Markus said, "Steffen is the key, but he never realized it fully. Until recently, I didn't know the truth about this wand. That truth will save us. However, at this time, I feel it necessary to keep my ultimate plan to myself. If the Dark Lady finds out by any means, then she could stop me before I get the opportunity I need. Again, I need you to trust me."

The three Lords looked at one another and then nodded in silent agreement. Lord Flavian said, "The fate of Gallenor is in your hands. What do you need from us?"

Markus smiled with eagerness. "Your planned attack is good, it will both distract her and give me an opening. However, as I said, you are unprepared for what you will encounter. This kind of dark war has not been waged since before the birth of Gallenor. The demons at her command are terrible. But there are others among us who do know them and have fought them. I think it's time we call upon some extra allies." He summoned his Dragonwand and slowly moved its tip over the table. A small wooden staff appeared, hardly bigger than a twig. He picked it up and held it out to Flavian.

Flavian was curious at first but quickly realized what he was being presented. Gently taking the staff, he said, "The gnomes?"

Markus nodded. "I will fly you to the gnome lands, you will use that amazing eloquence of yours to speak once again with Brek and Lord Brim. Ask for their assistance."

Flavian's smile grew. "It will be nice to speak with him again."

Markus said, "Yes. This time, you speak on behalf of all of Gallenor, and he will respect that... I hope. As for me, I will send a personal request to the Sea Fairies. They don't know me well, but they knew Tolen and Steffen."

Donna quietly asked, "Are you sure either of them will respond? The gnomes were almost wiped out and the Sea Fairies are rather snobbish, they don't care to meddle in human affairs."

Markus snorted. "All fairies are snobby. However, we both understand the impact of our loss. If the Dark Heart achieves full life and gains power through a Dragonwand core, no creature of any kind will escape the onslaught. You recall what happened to Alanor and Kirador."

Donna shivered. "They aren't even my memories and it still makes me want to cry when I think about the destruction of those lands."

Kellus asked, "Will that be enough if we have the united forces of Gallenor and the gnomes and fairies?"

Markus plainly stated, "No. There wouldn't be enough if we had every last man, woman, and child across Gallenor fighting. The dark creatures aren't mortal; they consist of shadows spun into demonic forces. They can be destroyed, but she can make more. Her legions are inexhaustible. However, our goal is not to defeat her army, it is to get this wand into Steffen's hands one last time. That is all that truly matters."

Everyone fell silent as this sank in. Lord Flavian finally spoke, "Markus...Lord Dragon. You're asking for a great deal of blind faith and trust here. Can you promise that this has a chance of success?"

Markus looked around the table. "We have already done something that no one has ever done in a fight against her."

"What?" Donna asked.

"Refuse to hate each other. While my assessment of her power is grim, the truth is we already won the first battle. She always sowed discord and hatred among people so they would fight each other first. It almost worked against us, but we stopped her. Now, on the eve of our most important battle against her, this land is united. This table is surrounded by the voice of every corner of Gallenor. This may not seem like a weapon, but it is. This is a light that will shine in her darkness. That, my friends, is a victory we can hold high as we march."

Kellus said, "We will remind all our troops of this. It will inspire greatness among them."

Flavian asked, "Then, what do we do next, Lord Dragon?"

"Tell your fighting men and women to give it their all; that is all we can ask. Tell me, what was your planned time to depart for the north?"

Kellus said, "Lord Shashla'yar, Captain Alex, and I will lead our troops toward the Shlan mountains for the Broken Ridge pass.

Donna was going to prepare a special potion for us and meet us in the Shlan lands in two days."

Shashla'yar added, "From the ridge, we can sssee the ancient wreck. I suspect that is where we will make our ssstand."

Markus nodded to them. "Then, go. Lord Flavian, we will leave for the Barren Mountains tomorrow morning. Please be ready."

"Yes, Lord Dragon."

***

Markus spent over three hours composing a short letter. He needed to choose just the right words to convince the Sea Fairies of the dire nature of the situation. Additionally, he had to write it in Fairy Script, a language and writing style that is extremely complicated and quite difficult to master. If it were written in any other form, they would not even read it, as it would insult their delicate customs. If Tolen hadn't had so many dealings with the Wood Fairies, Markus wouldn't know the first thing about writing in this language.

"That should do it." He finished the last bit of scrollwork on the edge of the last letter. He sat back and rubbed his tired hands. "It's a beautiful language, but boy is it hard to write." He folded the paper just right and sealed it with a special signet designed for him as the Dragon. Pressing it into a dripped amount of wax, he cast a spell, and the letter turned to mist. It flew through the walls and was on its way. "I hope they get that in time."

A light tapping came to his door. "Markus, are you in there?" Crystal's sweet voice asked.

With eagerness, he replied, "Please, come in."

She came through the door and approached him. "Is it true?"

"Is what true?"

"Treb told me that he and Kiin are leaving with the other armies right away for the north."

"Yes. That's the plan. Donna and I will join them later, as we can fly. I hate to allow Kiin to go in her condition, but she is still a good fighter and we need her."

Crystal frowned at him. "So, are you taking me with you or am I going to go with Donna?"

Markus let out a soft sigh. "I already told you that you wouldn't be going."

"What! I am so going! You need me."

"It's going to be too dangerous."

Crystal pointed a clawed finger at him. "That's what you said about the battle here, and I helped you, didn't I? If I hadn't come out, you'd be dead. We'd all be dead. So, I can help!"

Markus stood and took her hand, then grasped her other hand and held them together in his. "I can't let you go. You... you are a great wizard and a wonderful person. But you aren't fully trained in battle. This won't be like anything you've faced before. This will be terrible, immense, and dangerous. Besides, I have another job for you."

Through angry, pursed lips, she asked, "What would that be?"

"I'm sending you and the other elderly wizards to the college to care for everyone. The instructors are joining the armies as they pass through, which will leave only the students and the elderly. They will need someone responsible to remain there with them."

Crystal was almost growling. "That's just an excuse to get rid of me. You can't do this to me. I can't watch you go into battle while I sit at home and wait. I just can't."

"You have to. I'm giving you a direct order as the Lord Dragon and your boyfriend. I love you so much that I can't watch you go into a battle that will take your life."

Her stern, angry face quivered and melted into sorrow. "What if it takes your life? What if I never see you again? Oh..." She buried her face in him, crying. "Please, let me come and help you. I can protect you."

Markus held her close. "I'm doing this to protect you. I'm the Lord Dragon...I can handle this battle."

"You're a stupid, seventeen-year-old boy, that's what you are. And you're tearing my heart out right now." She bawled.

Markus patted her back. "I didn't mean to make you cry like this. Please, don't cry."

"I can't help it. I'm so scared right now. Everything is covered in taint, the world is about to end to some horrible woman from the past, and the man I love is heading right into the thick of it. I am so scared it hurts."

Markus continued to hold her, never wanting to let her go. "I don't have to leave until the morning. Let's just spend this evening together. Kissing, eating, being two teenagers in love and nothing else."

She cried as she said, "I'd like that."

***

The Dark Lady sat on her throne, Korvarsk at her right and Kellen on her left. She simply stared at the Dragonwand core floating across the room from her. The man behind the core hung limp in the air, the light magic flowing out of him hardly a trickle now.

Kellen was awakened from where he had fallen asleep when she stood. Both he and Korvarsk timidly watched her walk directly for the core. Kellen couldn't stop looking at her tail, as she had a rather long one now that she looked like Alieth.

Gently caressing the Dragonwand core, the look on her face grew cold. "This is not right."

Korvarsk came halfway to her and nervously asked, "What is wrong, my lady?"

"The magic from Steffen is almost spent, and yet the core is hardly ready. It still resists the darkness."

Kellen asked, "What can this mean?"

Steffen lifted his head to this, though it took great effort. The Dark Lady never took her eyes off the core. She answered, "I don't know. This should work unless..." her gaze turned to Steffen, "unless the light in you is no longer strong enough."

Steffen, appearing as though he would fall asleep at any moment, mocked her, "Or, perhaps, your grand scheme has flaws."

Approaching him, she grabbed his face in her hand. "I do not make mistakes."

"Oh, yes you do. By the time you realize it, I will be gone and your hope for supreme power will be nothing more than a failed dream." He managed a weak laugh.

She slapped him so hard it jostled the huge chains. "Do not presume to be anything more than a tool in here. I will not be mocked by you." Her outburst made both Korvarsk and Kellen take a few steps back. Leaving him to his pain, she walked toward the large windows as she spoke aloud. "The light exists, it has to. Only the true light could have cast a purification spell strong enough to clear a whole city." She stopped and looked out over her growing army of dark minions.

Korvarsk came closer, though kept his distance. "How was the city purified? Who did it?"

She spent a long time watching the monsters milling about on the ground below her. Finally, she said, "The boy."

"What?" Korvarsk frowned.

"In that moment, while I was controlling your form, I battled that awful woman with the Dragonwand. Suddenly, a wave of pure light magic struck me. It briefly expelled me from your mind, but just before I left, I saw that boy casting a spell. Until now, I thought he was just holding that damned candle in place. But now I believe he was the true caster of the spell. He was the source of the light that purified the town."

"No," Steffen rasped. "I cast that spell. It was mine."

She returned to him and leaned over to look at his face. "A liar now, are we? This child, this boy with the Dragonwand. He reminds me of someone. When I first met him on my ship, I knew he was more than just another human wizard. He has Tolen's wisdom and looks, but...he has your heart. The boy must be your heir, your bloodline."

Steffen closed his eyes and said nothing.

She laughed. "You are correct, I did make a mistake. I failed to realize who my true enemy is. How foolish of you to place so much trust and faith in a mere child. If you could lose to me, what do you expect him to do? Oh, this is delightful. I will enjoy tearing the light from him as I took it from you."

"No," Steffen whispered.

The Dark Lady turned sharply to Korvarsk. "I need the use of your body again."

Korvarsk summoned his Dragonwand and bowed. "As you wish."

"Look!" Kellen yelled out and pointed toward the windows.

A large horde of imps flew toward them. The Dark Lady cocked her head as she watched them approach. "Those aren't of my creation; mine are black, but these are purple and green."

Kellen said, "The imps of the Barren Mountains are purple and the imps of the Blue Forests are green. These are the wild dark creatures that normally stay in the land. What are they doing up here?"

Korvarsk added, "And why do they come like a Dragon was chasing them?"

The Dark Lady approached a window and extended her hand. "I shall find out." A streak of purple lightning shot from her and struck one of the imps, quickly pulling it to her. She seized it by its disgusting skull, and in an instant, its body burst apart and transformed into fine mist. She absorbed the mist and took a moment to assess it. A wicked smile spread across her face. "I see, I see. How delightful. It seems that we won't need to search for the boy; he will be coming to us."

"What did you see?" Korvarsk asked.

She returned to her throne, only answering after she sat down. "A large army approaches, coming through the Shlan lands and over the Barren Mountains. It seems that those who the beautiful taint has not infected are marching right to us."

"Are you sure this boy will be with them?" Kellen asked.

"I have no doubt. I've seen this war before, fought it many times. Only, this time I will have what I never had before, a Dragon's form." She spoke loudly for Steffen's sake, "How wonderful for you. You shall see your progeny one last time as I rip the light from his soul and lay the drained husk of his body at your feet."

Korvarsk asked, "Why not just kill him and be done? He is of no use to you now."

"No. Causing him pain is a pleasure I will delight in for as long as I can. He has evaded me for centuries, plotted against me, and stopped my grand plan far too often. Now, when all his machinations fail and I am finally triumphant, I want him alive to witness his failure."

***

Strong winds blustered around Lord Flavian and Crystal from their perch on the back of Markus in his Dragon form. The ominous clouds of the skies depressed the colors of the world below as they approached the college.

"Is everyone doing fine?" Lord Flavian called out at the top of his lungs.

Elderly wizards filling a carriage waved and nodded at the Lord. The carriage was currently in the claws of Markus who transported them with as much care as he could.

Getting closer to the college, the slightly blue magical dome covering it became visible. There were hovering candles throughout the grounds, which surprised both Markus and Crystal.

"Okay, hold on, I'll make this as gentle as I can," Markus announced, placing the cart on the ground near the college. It was a rocky drop off, but not too bad. Markus then landed and lowered himself down so both his passengers could dismount.

Lord Flavian was right over to the cart to lend a helping hand to the elderly as they disembarked. His gallant nature never ceased to amuse Markus.

"Lord Dragon!" Cranshk called out, his familiar voice echoing.

Markus transformed into his human form and led Crystal to the edge of the barrier where Cranshk and Vulshk waited. Rema cast a spell to open a hole in the barrier so the people could come through. Markus greeted, "It's good to see you safe and healthy. I was worried when I first heard about the taint spreading. After watching the wizards go crazy in Thendor, I imagined the worst."

Vulshk said, "We got as many as we could here. Only a few were tainted and had to be dealt with."

Crystal quickly asked, "What about my parents?"

Both Shlan twins grew grim. Neither wanted to say anything.

Rema greeted them quietly, "My Lord Dragon, Lady Crystal, it is good to see you."

Crystal asked again, "What about my parents? Are they here?"

Rema frowned in sorrow. "Your parents were tainted and went mad. I had to paralyze them before they did any harm. They are in the ward set up in the Blue Forest, but I suspect everyone is in there by now. That taint spread faster than anything I have ever witnessed."

Markus calmly held Crystal's hand and said, "They'll be all right. I learned this morning that the taint has overtaken the Valley, which means my parents are down, too. But we can fix this. That is what I'm going to do."

"Oh, Markus. I'm so sorry," Rema said.

Markus set his jaw firmly, stating, "It just gives me more reason to succeed."

Crystal turned to him, begging, "Please, take me with you! I can't just stay here. I have to help. My parents are in dire trouble now, I have to help!"

Markus stepped back. "No. I will not change my mind on this. I need you to stay here. You need to look after Kiin and Trebs' baby."

"Anyone can look after a baby. I want to look after you."

Vulshk gasped. "Crystal isn't going with you? But, when the armies came by, they accepted all the wizards we could spare who could fight. Crystal would be very able to fight."

Before Crystal could continue to argue, Markus asked Rema, "Did they take any students?" His tone was both concerned and slightly angry.

"Only instructors and adults gathered from the forests. I had to hold Jehu back, he was determined to go." Jehu was the best magical combat student in the school, and always ready to test his skills in the line of duty.

Markus now firmly commanded, "You will go in there and wait. When this is over, I am sure we will need your medical expertise."

Crystal sniffed as another wave of crying hit her and reached out to take his hand. "At least kiss me goodbye."

Markus didn't need another invitation; he accepted this and gave her one last, grand kiss. Both twins turned away in embarrassment, while Rema merely grinned. Once they parted, Markus squeezed her hand and left, saying nothing more.

Lord Flavian followed him out, where they would return to the skies for their part. Flavian stopped when he nearly ran into Markus. "Oh, sorry. Are you going to transform into... are you okay?" he noticed the tears on Markus' face.

"I want to bring her with me. I want to let her fight. But I can't do it. I have to be strong."

Flavian whispered, "A good leader knows that sometimes the decisions are only for the best intentions. She will be safe here."

Markus walked away and transformed into a Dragon. He lowered himself, and Flavian took his place on Markus's back. They flew off into the skies with Crystal watching them all the way.

Rema reached through the hole in the barrier and took Crystal by the hand. "Honey, please come in; this hole will seal itself soon."

Crystal wiped her eyes and walked through the hole in the barrier. "I love him, but he can be so frustrating sometimes."

Rema laughed. "Welcome to the world of relationships. I think it's beautiful how much he loves you."

"I think he's stupid."

Cranshk and Vulshk walked into the college and toward the center square with Rema and Crystal. Jehu walked the elderly wizards over to a series of chairs, benches, and some cots set out under an overhanging roof in the gardens. They all sat down with weariness, letting out deep sighs. Several students brought over blankets and pillows to help them. Other students gathered in the middle of the square, solemnly chatting with worry etched into their young faces. One of the older students attempted to lighten the mood by reading out of a novel to the others. The entire area was tinted slightly by the barrier that covered the school. The old candlemaker sat with the elderly. She still held Kiin and Trebs little girl in her arms.

Crystal asked, "How is this barrier staying up like this? I've never seen one cast like this before."

Vulshk elbowed her brother, "It was his idea."

"Sort of. I had an idea and Vulshk came up with the barrier."

Crystal asked, "What was the idea?"

Rema answered, "I needed a way to cast this barrier so it would be strong and remain intact for a long time. I knew of an ancient barrier spell that wards off taint and darkness, but it wouldn't be strong enough to cover this whole school. Then this brilliant boy brought up the spellwick candles."

Crystal asked, "You had the recipe? The map with it is back in Thendor."

Cranshk shook his head. "I didn't need the map. I wrote it down when you read it aloud."

"I remember, you did write it down. Good thinking." Crystal patted him on the shoulder.

Vulshk nodded. "He has been writing everything down and keeping notes when anyone speaks about magic. He's gathered loads of wisdom. He wants to be just like his hero." She was pestering him.

"What's wrong with writing down good ideas and spells?" Cranshk defended.

Crystal frowned. "Markus is nothing like that. All his knowledge and wisdom come from that Dragonwand. He hardly writes things down, which can get annoying with how much he knows. On the other hand, I have to read extensively just to keep up."

Vulshk said, "Which is why you're his hero, not Markus."

Cranshk would be blushing right now as he glared at his twin sister, though Shlan scales never really show blushing. "Not a hero, just learning using the same method that another great wizard used. Crystal, you are a book-reading, note-taking wizard, so I'm going to do that too."

Crystal smiled. "I'm happy to be a role model for anyone."

Cranshk said, "I have a lot to prove as a Shlan wizards. So few of us exist, I can't slack on my studies."

Crystal nodded with a proud look in her eyes. "Logical. Now... what's all this?"

They walked out into the large open courtyard in the middle of the school. Large deflated balloons tethered to baskets were set about.

Vulshk answered, "These are the balloons we rode into visit the Knowing Oak."

"I know that," Crystal replied. "What are they doing out here?"

Rema shrugged. "Just a thought. If something bad happens and this barrier comes down, we could be attacked by rogue tainted wizards, imps, or other nasty stuff. This place isn't exactly a fortress.

If we need to escape, flying away would be better than trying to run, especially with the younger children or the elderly. I know I can't run like I used to."

"Interesting...very interesting." Crystal walked among the baskets and deflated balloons, pondering something deeply.

Vulshk asked, "What? They're just the traveling balloons."

Crystal stopped and looked up at the floating candles. "It might work, it will work."

"What?" Rema asked.

Crystal asked them, "Do you want to sit here and wait to hear how the battle comes out? Or do you want to do something about it?"

Rema was aghast. "Are you suggesting we go into battle?"

"No...well, yes."

Rema put her foot down. "No! Markus was wise in putting us here. The elderly and young are not ready or able to fight this war. We are safe here."

"For now long?" Crystal shot back, her words coming out fiercely.

"Until the battle is over." Cranshk stated with a lot of curiosity in his voice.

Crystal looked up at the boiling clouds in the sky. "Listen to me. If we win the battle and Markus returns home to me, then the world will be safe again. However, if he doesn't, then this place is not safe enough to protect us. This barrier will not outlast eternal darkness. This battle will decide the fate of all of us, whether or not we are present. I, for one, would rather help than just wait."

An elderly man walked over and pulled out his wand. "I know I speak for many of my piers here. We don't want to sit and simply wait for death. If I am going to die, I want to do it by facing down the enemy."

Rema appeared to be struggling as she considered this. "I have a duty to protect you. Markus... "

"Is just a seventeen-year-old boy who, for all his wisdom, can be an idiot some days." Crystal said, to the shock of those around her. "Markus has a good heart, this is why he is such a great hero. Sometimes that heart goes too far. He is protecting all of us. Markus doesn't even realize that if he fails, this school and this barrier will mean nothing."

Jehu called out from across the courtyard, "I would rather fight than wait for death!"

Rema looked around, all the faces now staring at her. "I... agree. We have to do something more than sit and wait. But how can we do anything from here? As I said, we are young or infirm. This war is happening in the far north."

Crystal gave off a clever smile. "I have a plan."

CHAPTER 5: STARING DOWN THE ENEMY

MARKUS flew over the Shlan Mountains near Broken Ridge Pass. He was alone, having already dropped off Flavian with the Gnomes. Most people did not use this pass, as few had reasons to venture this far north. On the other side of the pass was a steep decline leading down to the flat, desolate plains of the wastelands, home to many dark creatures on any given day and, at present, a haven for a vast dark army. Currently, hundreds of men and women were camped near the pass, not yet having crossed it.

It was not the pass or the army that caught Markus's attention; it was what loomed high over the skyline. A new, ominous structure rose into the clouds. Its pitch-black surface glistened in the sunlight. Swarms of terrible creatures flew around it. On the ground below, there were more shadow minions than Markus had ever seen, even from the memories within him of Tolen. Vicious fast looking creatures with gaping maws filled with sharp, dripping fangs. Lumbering giant monstrosities with tree trunk thick legs and hammer-like fists ready to crush. The imps were beyond count and among them flew unspeakable birds with spears for talons and screams that scratched the air throughout the land. Hungry shadow wolves prowled among the horrid legions, hunched and ready to rip into the flesh of any who dared to get close. This was a dark army unlike anything this world had experienced.

"What is that?" He squinted as he glided toward the ridge.

In the distance, behind the throngs of shadow creatures, there was what appeared to be pure darkness. Strange new mountains stood, blocking the ice peaks of the far north. They had little definition and rose higher than anything, save the dark palace. Then, they moved. These huge creatures weren't mountains; they were monsters of shadow. Nearly as tall as the massive spires of the dark castle next to them, these things were golems of mists and pitch-black energy.

Quickly descending before passing the ridge, Markus swooped low and transformed just as he touched the ground. There was only the mountain pass between the armies of Gallenor and the forces of the Dark Lady. It was unclear to Markus if the armies of shadow knew that just behind this ridge was their enemies. Markus left his concerns about this behind and joined the others. Nearby stood dozens of ranking members from all three armies, with Shashla'yar, Kellus, and Captain Alex at the center. Donna was near a vat of liquid, filling buckets with it. Soldiers approached, dipping cloth into the liquid before wiping it across their blades and armor. It imparted a unique sheen to whatever it washed over. Markus recognized a magical potion blend, which would require a further enchantment to activate. He wasn't clear exactly what Donna was using, but trusted her wisdom as a potion master with ancient knowledge.

Markus approached Donna first, a curious expression on his face. "What are you doing with that potion?"

She handed a bucket to a young Shlan warrior who promptly left in a hurry. "Doling out this potion, what does it look like?"

"You mentioned a potion back at Thendor. What kind of potion?"

She tilted her head at him for a moment and then realized something. "Ah, right. You weren't at the entire planning meeting. This is a brightness potion with a spell activator. They are applying it all over their weapons and armor. When we go into battle, the wizards will cast a brightness charm on them, and the potion will illuminate. You know, to mess with those dark creatures."

Markus lifted both eyebrows. "Good idea. It won't really hurt them much, but it will distract them."

"That's the idea. Any tactical advantage is a welcome one right now. Did you see that army?"

Markus nodded. "Yes. It's terrible."

"And those giants...I know my Dragonwand doesn't remember anything like that."

"Tolen hasn't seen anything like that before, either. We cannot forget that our enemy has been around longer than the Dragonwands. She will have considered new strategy, new weapons."

Donna dipped a ladle into the potion and finished another bucket for a Rakki warrior. "We will be as ready as we can be."

Alex, Kellus, and Shashla'yar came over. "Our scouts have reported that an innumerable army waits for us on the other side of these mountains," Kellus stated.

Alex added, "Among them are creatures we have never encountered before. I've fought imps, but never shadow horses, trolls, or giants."

"At least I know where Steffen is," Markus stated flatly, his gaze turning to the dark palace.

Alex pointed at the pass. "Did you hear us? That army is beyond our ability to fight."

"I heard you, I saw it myself. We are not alone in this. Trust me."

Donna said, "The Dark Lady has to know we're here and about to invade. Her forces are all poised for attack, they are in lines waiting for us. I'm surprised she hasn't come for us yet."

Markus said, "I'm sure she has her plan. She is waiting for us to strike."

Alex asked, "Is this all a trap? Are we leading our armies to their doom?"

Donna said, "It is certainly part of her plan. She is ready for us. However, I know from my own knowledge of her past actions, she is biding her time until she has gained the power she desires. If we retreat now and change plans, it will only give her time. "

"I won't give her the time. This has to end, Gallenor is near extinction from the taint as it is. Trap or no trap, we must attack. She may have her plans, but we have ours. We must trust in them." Markus said, then asked, "Are your forces ready?"

"They have the potion on their weapons and armor," Donna stated.

Each commander gave a short nod to the other, and then Shashla'yar answered for them, "Our forces are almost in formation."

"Good. I'll go in first and call her out. Be ready to charge as soon as you see my signal." Markus turned and headed for the pass.

Kellus asked, "What is the signal?"

"You'll know."

On the other side, looking down at the vast northern wastelands, Markus paused at the sight of the pulsing armies of shadow, ready to tear him apart. Instead of walking down, he transformed into a Dragon and glided, landing just before lines of drooling minions. He shifted back to his human form and stood calmly. As if in no danger, he knelt and placed his hand on the ground, feeling it momentarily. With a satisfied smile, he stood.

He held up his Dragonwand and spoke across the top of it, his voice booming with aid of magic, "LADY OF DARKNESS! I

HAVE COME FOR STEFFEN AND KORVARSK! SHOW YOURSELF!"

The dark minions cackled, growled, and made other strange noises, their eyes greedy for the chance to destroy him. A long moment of hesitation passed as nothing happened. Then, a Dragon's roar echoed from the castle, and Korvarsk flew out of the highest tower. Markus stood firm, gripping his Dragonwand. The enemy Dragon dropped swiftly and then flew closer over the shadow army. With a hard thud, Korvarsk landed in front of Markus. He assumed his Shlan form, holding his Dragonwand.

"What makes you think I want to be saved?" Korvarsk asked.

Markus's expression did not change from unimpressed. "Don't try to fool me, lady. I know it is you in him."

Korvarsk's face gradually morphed into a vicious smile, horrifying on a Shlan's serpentine lips. "How clever and brash you've become. You truly are the heir of Tolen and Steffen—just as handsome and just as arrogant."

"I'm proudly the descendant of Steffen and Tolen; they were both great men, and Steffen still is. Though, he does not fully realize it yet."

Korvarsk circled around Markus. "How fitting that we should conclude this here. It was here that you and I first met. I should thank you, young Markus of the Valley. You broke the barrier that kept me at bay for so long. You and this boy entered my sanctum, eager to learn the secrets of darkness. I would have ended you then, had Steffen not intervened."

"You caught me by surprise. I had truly never seen anything like you before. But, I'm stronger, smarter, and more determined than ever to find the answers to defeating darkness."

"You are stronger. You have the light in you... I need that. So, I should thank you for bringing it to me." Korvarsk stopped and stood in front of Markus, threateningly close.

Markus smiled at him. "I won't go so easily. This time, I'm ready to face you."

Korvarsk laughed. "Oh, with your pitiful army. I've already seen it. I have faced bigger forces before, stronger forces. This will be a bloodbath. I will garner much strength from it and rid myself of a few pests."

Markus retained his smile. "No, you haven't faced a force like this before."

She grew angrier at him. "Your arrogance is becoming annoying."

"Not arrogance, just reality. You have inflicted great wars over the thousands of years you have been around. But, you truly have not faced a force like mine. For, you see, this time the force is united. The strength is one. You may have more numbers, but you lack in true strength. I am not just the Dragon, I am of Gallenor, and behind me, around me, with me, are the united people of Gallenor, fighting as one. There is no dissension, no civil war this time. You failed to cause that. Your greatest tactic has failed you, what makes you think you can win? We stand united, we stand as one."

Furious, she barked, "What foolish words from a foolish child! What can weak humans, snakes and dogs do to the likes of me!"

"Oh, there is so much more than that facing you."

Korarsk hissed at Markus, "What, you want to bluff me into surrendering? Is this your game?"

Markus shook his head. "Not at all. I just needed some time, and I know how much you love to bluster and boast. But I think my friends are almost here so... ECHO!" He thrust his wand forward and sent a massive shockwave at Korvarsk, sending him tumbling through the front lines of the shadow minions.

Behind Markus, the pass and ridge came alive with soldiers running down. The humans and Rakki used the paths, the Shlan crawled across the surface.

Korvarsk leaped into the air, transforming into a Dragon, and yelled, "Rip them apart!"

Markus transformed quickly and flew up, avoiding being mauled by ten shadow wolves in front of him. He screamed a roar filled with electricity and showered the front lines with magic, dissolving many foes in one strike.

Donna appeared over the ridge, flying across the surface and bellowing a spell as she did so. The allied armies lit up with bright light. Their swords, armor, arrows, and even some of their skin were now aglow with a brilliant white magical light. The denizens of the Darkness faltered in their assault, blinded by this brilliance.

The first allies to reach the battle were the swift Shlan forces. They crashed into the lines of wolves and other man-sized creatures. The Shlan employed their short swords and blades, deftly moving through their enemy lines and cutting down many as they attacked.

Arrows rained down over the fields, picking off dozens of imps in moments. Rakki archers, now clinging to the sides of the mountains, took aim and eliminated the vast airborne legions under the Dark Lady's control.

Finally, the united human and Rakki foot armies descended and joined the battle. The wizards fought alongside the blade-wielding non-wizards. Their magic was mainly defensive, but they collaborated with the warriors beside them.

Markus and Donna flew right at Korvarsk, all three Dragons in the air, the raging battle on the ground below. Markus shot first, hitting Korvarsk in a wing, causing him to crash into the ground before getting airborne again. Donna followed that with two fireballs from her hands, thrown at Korvarsk. He dodged both of them, allowing them to obliterate part of the rushing army of trolls below.

Korvarsk made a large curve in the sky, screaming a spell that sent a wave of power across the dark clouds. However, it did nothing to Markus or Donna, which confused them. He then came around, heading right for Markus and picking up speed.

"I WILL HAVE YOUR LIGHT!" he yelled, shooting a barrage of dark energy at Markus.

Markus maneuvered in the air to avoid being hit, but he couldn't escape it and was struck in the face by a blast of dark magic. He skidded across the ground and was set upon by hundreds of shadow wolves. He punched, kicked, used his wings, and unleashed a fire blast to fend them off. Donna dove in to help him, but he shouted, "STOP KORVARSK!"

She arced back into the sky and went for Korvarsk, who was still set on attacking Markus. She flew right at him and dodged several spells sent her direction. With a quick change in her path, she grabbed his wing and yanked him off course. She swung him around and planted him on the ground with a hard throw. The impact caused Korvarsk to change back into himself for a moment. Now, surrounded by hundreds of the shadow army, Korvarsk pulled himself up. Donna knew he would be airborne again soon, so she acted quickly. She dropped down, slammed into the earth, and unleashed her paralysis attack. The wave of magical energy radiated outward, stunning hundreds of trolls, wolves, and a few imps.

Korvarsk stood, shaken by the attack. Yet, he looked up at her with a smile. "You need to learn a bit more from that Dragonwand.

That spell doesn't work very well against other Dragons. However, I'm done dealing with you."

"Enough!" Donna gathered a surge of magic in her mouth and was about to unleash it when a massive ball of shadow energy struck her in the chest, sending her crashing through shadow warriors and allies. When she finally came to a stop, she groaned and looked up to see what had hit her. The towering monsters were now moving, their enormous hands gathering shadow magic and hurling it across the field. She had only a split second to get out of the way before three more attacks struck her where she lay. The ground erupted when the blasts hit; she dodged the impact but not the aftermath. The shockwave sent her tumbling again, though not as violently this time. In that moment, she lost control of her Dragon form and reverted to her true self.

"Donna!" The voice of Treb surprised her. He came running with Kiin and five other Rakki warriors at his side. They were all aglow with her potion magic.

"Treb! Where are the others?" She looked at his tiny forces.

Kiin swung her twin blades through the air, slicing an imp in half with a single strike. Then she answered, "Killed. We've lost most..." She paused, eliminating another imp. "We've lost most of our people already."

Treb used his blue sword to slice up several shadow wolves. "Get up. We need you!"

Donna got to her knees and was prepared to stand when she saw the lines of trolls racing toward them. There were hundreds against the seven of them. Behind them, one of those behemoths loped toward her. "I can't fight this," she whispered, the sound of defeat in her words..

Suddenly, the ground rumbled, but it wasn't from the giant footfalls of those behemoths or the lines of trolls. The earth shook, cracked, and made crunching noises. All at once, gnomes emerged from the ground, running with astonishing speed. As they moved, rocks and dirt gathered around them, encasing each one until the tiny gnome had transformed into a seven-foot rock warrior. They sped past the Rakki forces and confronted the trolls with agility and precision. The stone warriors wielded stone swords and clubs to crush skulls and cleave bodies in half. Some of the gnome warriors didn't use weapons; instead, they employed magic, summoning massive walls of spikes from the ground that killed dozens of trolls in single strikes.

One of the gnome warriors stopped by Donna and helped her up. The rocks moved in the chest, revealing a face. It was King Brek. "My Lady Dragon, how nice to meet you."

She brushed herself off and summoned her Dragonwand. "Am I glad to see you. If you can help the Rakki lines, I will see if I can stall that behemoth. I doubt I can take it down, it's three times the size of a Dragon."

Brek grinned. "Don't worry, we did not come alone."

At that moment, an earsplitting explosion shook the wastelands. Both armies paused just long enough to glance at the volcano and see that it was erupting. Lava spewed upward and spilled down the sides, while smoke belched high into the atmosphere. Then, something unexpected occurred. The entire mountain exploded as a massive warrior made of lava broke through. As large as the behemoth, this rock and fire monster stormed through the battle, stomping on hundreds of trolls and wolves in its path. In a swift and decisive move, the lava man punched the behemoth, driving his fist right through the monster's head.

Donna yelled out, "WHAT IS THAT!"

Brek laughed. "That, my friend, is Lord Brim, King of the Gnomes. Now, I might suggest, we get back to the battle." His face was covered in stone again as he quickly sliced an imp in half that was dive bombing their position.

Donna realized that this new ally wasn't enough to turn the battle, there was still a lot of ground to cover. Brek had raced off to join the other gnomes and Rakki. The lines of enemies were approaching her quickly, but she had a moment. Closing her eyes briefly, she harnessed the deep memories of the greatest warrior Dragon ever.

She moved the Dragonwand around in careful patterns with a swift motion of her hands. Using her unique strength in earth magic, she thrust her hands forward and sent large energy waves into the earth. The rushing demons stumbled and were tossed around. Without missing a beat, she cut her hands from side to side, and in the waves, large spikes of rock jutted up quickly, piercing clean through trolls and wolves. With this dance of rocks, she sliced through dozens of shadow minions in seconds. Then came the buzzing, thousands of imps were rushing at her. She swiped her Dragonwand through the air, and the spikes of earth broke free, spiraling in the air like a giant cyclone. She mowed through the hordes of imps, popping hundreds every second. But, their numbers were so great that she was running out of spikes before they were upon her. However, she was ready. Just as the survivors got to her location, she suddenly held her arms against her, pressing her Dragonwand up to her chest. She slid straight down into the earth and avoided the shower of purple imp magic meant to obliterate her.

Suddenly, she burst back up through the earth, now as a Dragon. She crashed into the horde and decimated them. With a clear opening, she set her sights on the fight against Korvarsk, but she was stopped when two of those behemoths came at her, throwing their large shadow bombs in her direction.

Lord Kellus stood on the mountainside, using his bow to launch arrow after arrow. His unit of elite Rakki archers was assigned to imp control. Two Rakki wizards stood nearby, dipping arrows in potions and enchanting them to glow. They tossed the arrows to the archers, who quickly fired them into the battle, targeting either imps or other foes.

"Sir! There are too many imps!" One of the archers called out as she shot three arrows at once, hitting three different imps.

"That only means we can't miss," Kellus stated, then shot a bright glowing arrow through one imp and into another, both popping midair.

Suddenly, one of the behemoths hurled a shadow bomb at Donna, missed, and struck the mountain above their perch. Boulders began to roll down, creating a landslide. The agile, lightly armored archers skidded down the slope, hoping to escape their doom.

Donna flew by, shooting three fireballs at the behemoth, then turned and cast a spell over the landslide. The rocks hovered and stopped, and the dirt spread away from the people. However, just as she held this at bay, a blast of shadow magic struck her in the back and threw her against the ground. She lost her control, and the landslide resumed. Fortunately, she bought enough time for the Rakki to get away.

Donna was on the ground, dazed and in pain. Around her, the Rakki archers gathered, shooting arrows and fighting with knives. Hordes of shadow minions surrounded them.

"DONNA!" Kellus yelled as he shot at approaching trolls and imps.

She groaned, "My head."

Kellus stepped slightly on her back and aimed at the creature bearing down on them. "Donna! We need you." He shot, but his arrow merely stuck into the chest of the monster.

Donna was jolted back to reality as the thud of the creature's feet shook her. She looked up from where she was grounded and saw one of the wizards gripping the bucket of potion with one hand while using the other to cast spells at enemies. "YOU!" she yelled. "Throw that potion on me, now!"

The wizards pointed his wand, yelled, "HRINDA!" and sent a gale of wind at a swarm of approaching imps. Then he quickly rushed over and tossed the potion on Donna, mostly soaking her head. "Is that what you wanted?"

She smiled and slowly got up, careful not to hurt any of the defenders around her. "Precisely." She turned and looked up at the monster bearing down on them. She cast the light spell and continued to repeat it, the potion glowing ten times brighter than usual, illuminating her head and upper neck as brightly as the sun. The nearby shadow minions all recoiled at the brightness; even the Rakki were startled by it. She beat her wings, lifted into the air, and darted toward the behemoth. The monster leaned back, ready to smash her as she got close, but she was too fast. She compressed her wings against her sides, straightened her body as much as possible, and blasted clean through the head of the monster. It stumbled back, reaching for its missing body part, then fell backward, crushing a large segment of the dark army nearest the Rakki warriors.

Donna wasted no time. She went after the next behemoth that was not far behind its companion. Unfortunately, she had spent all the potion. The pure darkness of the monster countered the light on her, and it was washed off. But, she focused on the monster with her magic, blasting it and distracting it from throwing more shadow bombs at the allied forces.

Kellus stood stunned by what he had just witnessed. He shook it off, quickly pulled out his bow, and reached for an arrow from his quiver. There wasn't an arrow to be had. "Wizards, where are more arrows?"

The same wizard who assisted Donna approached, casting spells at the imps charging toward them. "The reserves were lost in the landslide, sir."

"Damn!" Kellus tossed his bow aside and drew his twin blades. A shadow troll charged at him. Kellus dodged its attacks twice, then drove a knife into its shoulder and swung around to bury the other in its neck. He yanked them both out and kicked the creature in the back. A wizard struck the troll with a lightning spell, killing it instantly.

The Rakki forces continued this dance with the approaching forces, hardly gaining any ground, but keeping them at bay.

CHAPTER 6: THE FALL OF A KING

EARLIER:

Markus was covered in shadow wolves, and they snapped at his wings and arms. Some tried biting directly into his flesh. But a dragon's body is many times more dense than the toughest skin in nature. Unfortunately, they were numerous and he couldn't get the upper hand.

Above him, he watched Donna get blasted by some shadowy ball and thrown away. The ground rumbled loudly and those huge behemoths moved into the thick of combat. Korvarsk hovered above him, casting a spell to darken the skies.

In a gleeful voice, Korvarsk announced, "And the downfall of this pitiful resistance comes. Kill them all my beautiful creations."

Markus roared with rage as the wolves almost wholly covered him. All he could think of was that Donna could be killed, their forces could be destroyed, the battle had barely begun, and it was already lost. "I will not lose! I will not let Gallenor FALL!" He screamed, and his body emitted light unlike Donna's potion spell. Only, this light was tinged with gold. This was the purifying light. The wolves on him were destroyed, the creatures nearest him were laid low, and Korvarsk was knocked out of the skies.

123

Korvarsk hit the ground and transformed back into a Shlan. He was near Markus. "You... you are far too dangerous, even though you don't fully know how to control that light. Korvarsk, bring him to me." He said this with his own mouth and then seemed to go into a daze for a second. Dark energy left his body and returned to the castle. In a moment, Korvarsk was once again glaring at Markus.

"Korvarsk... is it you?" Markus softly asked.

Korvarsk snarled and then ran at Markus, transforming into a Dragon. When he made contact, he grabbed Markus by the neck and carried him up and away. He bellowed at Markus with a mouthful of greenish hellfire.

Markus lurched back from the attack, his entire head engulfed by the flames. He reached out and grabbed Korvarsk with his claws and sent a massive jolt of thunder magic into Korvarsk. This blasted them apart, both smoldering from the other's attacks.

"You cannot win!" Korvask yelled. "You are far outnumbered!"

Markus was about to reply when they both saw a flash of orange light and heard an explosion. They turned to see the volcano explode and Lord Brim emerged from the flames as the giant lava warrior.

Markus laughed. "Told you I didn't come alone."

Korvarsk screamed and charged at Markus, randomly blasting him with fireballs and lightning. Markus dodged and flew away, staying ahead of Korvarsk. He attempted to turn and retaliate, but Korvarsk, consumed by rage, pushed forward with such intensity that it was impossible to pause for even a moment. All Markus could do was prevent Korvarsk from closing in on allied lines; otherwise, his numerous misses would prove devastating.

Suddenly, one of the behemoths hit the ground, and Donna flew by at an amazing speed. She nearly hit Korvarsk, interrupting his attack.

Markus used the delay and shot back. He hit Korvarsk in the face with a fireball and rushed him, grabbing his tail and throwing him to the ground. Korvarsk smashed into the shadow armies, obliterating a full line of shadow warriors. Not giving him a chance, Markus hit Korvarsk with a steady stream of energy, shoving him across the ground and through even more shadow warriors.

It seemed as though Korvarsk was defeated. He lay in a pile of dirt and debris, hardly moving. Markus would have the perfect opportunity to finish this, but he hesitated. Korvarsk looked up at the castle, clawed his way back up, got airborne, and flew away.

Markus saw the opening. Donna had the behemoths distracted, and the shadow forces were split. There was a clear path to the castle. All he had to do was follow it. Not considering anything but his objective, Markus raced after Korvarsk and made his way into the castle.

A team of his best warriors surrounded Lord Shashla'yar. Using a sword, he cut down dark warrior after warrior. His skill was amazing and his determination terrifying. Unfortunately, the Shlan numbers were dwindling.

"My Lord!" his first officer yelled as he sliced through two shadow warriors at once. "We are not going to make it!"

"It doesn't matter. We must fight until the end. There is no other choice!" Shashla'yar slashed two shadow trolls' heads off in one slice. He spun around and used his tail to trip a warrior, stabbing him in a fluid strike after finishing those trolls.

Just then, two more of his remaining Shlan fell, and he was standing with only his first officer. They fought vigilantly, moving from foe to foe. But, the darkness was encapsulating them.

Coming over the throng of shadow minions were furry warriors, stabbing and slashing with short blades. The Rakki forces broke through and joined Shashla'yar. Lord Kellus came up and saved the Shlan king by killing a troll nearly upon him.

Kellus came back to back with Shashla'yar. "Could you use some help?"

Shashla'yar laughed as he fought. "If you inssisst."

The two armies, Rakki and Shlan, fought side by side. Their unique fighting styles were balanced to work in tandem as they cut down foes and pushed back the lines against them.

"Look!" Kellus's first officer yelled. "Markus is at the castle."

Kellus smiled. "He made it."

"But we won't," Shashla'yar proclaimed as their foes once again surrounded them.

The two kings fought back-to-back. Kellus said, "I knew we would be in a war together one day."

"At leassst, we're on the sssame ssside," Shashla'yar replied with a grin.

"What is that?" the Shlan commander asked.

Kellus plunged his blades into the neck of an approaching troll, ripped them out, and kicked its carcass away. Then he looked up and saw five large balloons floating over the mountains.

ABOVE THEM:

Crystal was surrounded by students and some elderly wizards from the college. They sat in the balloon baskets and used magic to maneuver the balloons over the battle.

"They really did a good job fighting imps," Crystal said. "I thought we'd see a lot more of them."

Jehu pointed down at the battle. "Look, our forces are thin."

"What do we do?" Rema asked, trembling all over.

"What we can to weaken the darkness. Release the lanterns!"

Rema and Jehu each picked up a lantern with one of the spellwick candles attached. They ignited the flame using magic and then let it go. The heat from the candle kept it afloat as it drifted away from the balloon basket. Two candles were released from each of the other three baskets, and wizards in every basket used magic to push the lanterns as far apart as possible.

"Are you sure this will work?" Jehu asked.

"No, but I have hope. Rema, if you would."

Rema held up an antique spellbook and recited the old incantation to clear the rainy weather. She aimed her wand at the nearest candle. "Brynn Lopt! Brynn Lopt!..." She repeated this, and a blue spell was cast upon the candle. Each of the candles radiated this spell just as they had with the light spell before. The light expanded outward, forming a bluish-white glow. The few imps who had been interested in the balloons were sent fleeing by the brightness. Then, the dark clouds above the battle began to thin and fade away.

"It's working!" Crystal announced.

Jehu suddenly leaned over the side. "LORD KELLUS!"

"What?" Crystal looked down and sat on what appeared to be a fallen man.

"I'm going down!" Jehu didn't ask permission. He cast an anti-gravity spell on himself and jumped from the flotilla, practically gliding to the surface.

"GO, GO, GO!" Crystal called out and she followed Jehu.

The other students and a few of the elderly joined in. A stream of wizards flew down, heading for the front lines of the battle.

This display of magic transfixed Kellus. He did not see that shadow warrior bearing down on him with a long spear.

"WATCH OUT!" Shashla'yar pushed Kellus out of the way and received the spear meant for the Rakki Lord. It punctured him through his chest and went all the way to the other side.

Kellus quickly threw one of his blades and buried it in the shadow warrior's forehead, dissolving him. "Shashla'yar!" He yelled out and dropped to his knees.

At that moment, the college student wizards jumped down from the balloons and joined the combined Rakki and Shlan forces. The kids didn't fight as much as they defended, pushing the enemy back.

"KELLUS!" Crystal came running over.

Kellus was beside Shashla'yar, holding him. "Crystal! Oh, thank goodness. Please, help him!"

She gasped at the sight of who lay on the ground. She quickly cast a spell over him but then hesitated. A painful pause gripped her breathing as she struggled to say, "I... I can't help him."

Kellus leaned in, gazing at Shashla'yar's face. "My old friend, why did you do it?"

Shashla'yar had blood trickling out of his mouth and his breathing was shallow. He coughed and rasped out, "I had to. I...I failed Gallenor...you are a good man. Gallenor needsss you."

Kellus had tears in his eyes. "You are a good man. I never doubted that once."

Shashla'yar weakly grabbed Kellus' hand. "Win...today. Pleassse." His grip loosened and his head fell to the side. There wasn't any life left in him.

Kellus turned his sorrow into fury. He reached over to pick up Shashla'yar's sword. "We will win," he declared. He got up and rushed to the front lines, fighting alongside Rakki, Shlan, and the wizards. They were vastly outnumbered, but they were fueled by a courage that the shadow could not possibly fathom.

CHAPTER 7: THE THRONE OF DARKNESS

MARKUS raced past the surging dark minions, his sights set on Korvarsk. The dragon in front of him arched into the sky as he approached the Obsidian Castle, heading for the grand windows. Markus followed suit, inching closer with each passing second.

Finally, Korvarsk flew through a large open window, transforming mid-flight and landing on the floor as a Shlan. Markus followed closely behind him, transforming in midair before touching down on his feet. Without missing a beat, he thrust his Dragonwand forward and shouted, "ECHO!" A shockwave hit Korvarsk, sending him sprawling across the ground.

"Steffen!" Markus spotted the man suspended in the center of the room, bound to the walls by magical chains. A thread of energy flowed from him directly into the core of the Dragonwand.

"No... Markus... go..." Steffen weakly tried to warn Markus.

Markus swiped his Dragonwand through the air, severing one of the chains that connected Steffen's right arm to the wall. He aimed to do the same with the right leg when a blast of wind struck him, slamming him against a wall. He saw Korvarsk casting this wind. Markus raised his wand and called out, "HLIF!" A barrier formed between him and Korvarsk. The wind cut around the small, invisible field, giving Markus room to stand. "Don't fight me, Korvarsk. I don't want to hurt you."

Korvarsk hissed and yelled, "Too bad, because I want to kill you! PRYMJA!" He summoned a lightning bolt from the tip of his wand and shot Markus's barrier, breaking it.

Markus tumbled to the side, avoiding the second bolt of lightning summoned by Korvarsk. Sliding on the ground, he yelled, "HRINDA!" and sent Korvarsk flying into a wall. Korvarsk went down, knocked out by the blow to his head. Markus waited long enough to see that Korvarsk wasn't getting back up. "That...was easier than I thought," he muttered. "No time to dwell on it. Steffen!" He quickly got to his feet and rushed back to save Steffen.

"No, Markus, please. You have to go." Steffen fought fatigue as he said this.

Markus released Steffen's other arm. The energy connection to Steffen was severed, halting the flow into the core. Markus caught Steffen before he fell to the ground. "What did she do to you?"

"Leave me," Steffen croaked.

"No. Here, I brought you this." Markus pulled out Steffen's wand and handed it to him.

Steffen feebly looked at the wand. "What...why did you bring this to me?"

"You... GAH!" A bright blast of energy hit Markus in the back, and he was pulled away and knocked against the ground.

The Dark Lady stepped out of the shadows, her hand extended where she had struck Markus. "Oh, how precious. Your grand and glorious plan was to bring Steffen his old wand. That's it? His light is almost gone, and you don't know how to use yours. What did you think, that the two of you would be enough to stop me? Such a foolish strategy. Here, I expected more from the heir of Tolen's supposed wisdom." Markus turned over and grabbed his fallen Dragonwand. She held her hand out before he could raise it again and struck him once more, this time longer and harder. He screamed in pain, writhing on the ground. Finally halting the flow of energy, she laughed. "How you forget. In this darkness, in this place, I have greater power than you. I almost destroyed you when we first met on that accursed ship. Now, in a palace of darkness, I am even stronger.

Markus struggled against the residual pain. "It's over. You can't win this time."

"Oh, but I already have." She pointed at him, and a bright white energy struck his chest. She screamed just as loudly as he did when this began. Directing it toward the floating core, she established the connection. The light emerged from Markus as a brilliant glow but was filtered through her darkness, transforming into a curse within the core. Releasing her grip on the drain, it continued on its own.

"No, Markus!" Steffen raised his wand, but was met with a blast of dark shadow energy. He was thrown to the ground in nearly a prostrate position. Kellen lifted the Pearl and cast this wicked spell at him through it.

133

Markus was lifted into the air as the energy drained from him. With a quick swipe of her hands, chains materialized once more, wrapping around his arms and legs. She stepped closer. "You were so easily manipulated. Korvarsk led you right to me. Awww, and you thought you were winning." She smiled while Korvarsk kindly stood and dusted himself off, obviously unharmed.

Grunting under the extreme agony, Markus said, "What? But..."

"But...but..." she mocked. "My forces could have crushed you already. Oh, your little armies put up quite a valiant fight. But it is truly hopeless; nothing can stop me now." She gripped the core, the energy flowing right through her fingers into it. "Now, with the true light, twisted and corrupted, I will have ultimate power. Even now, while it's only half complete, I will demonstrate the kind of control I will wield as the first Dragon of Shadow." She looked up, and the room grew darker. The skies outside, which had been cut by the candle magic, thickened like oil. A terrible darkness spread across all of Gallenor, not from clouds, but as if the sky itself had become darkness. Following that, the din of her minions blossomed into a mighty roar, accompanied by the earth-shaking footfalls of more of those behemoths climbing out of the shadow.

The college students fought with all their strength. They blocked spells from the imps and sent shockwaves to push the enemies back. The more experienced wizards were casting powerful wind spells, tossing the front lines into those behind them. They couldn't pause long enough to cast a destructive spell.

Jehu charged right into the front lines with a handful of something. He hurled it at the enemy, showering them with strange, diamond-like crystals. It had no effect. The enemy pressed on as he patiently waited. Suddenly, he cast a simple water spell at them, and all the crystals erupted in torrents of liquid. These were Donna's renowned condensed water crystals.

He commanded the water to flow, a massive surge of liquid tossing dark creatures around and smashing them into one another. Finally, with a thrust of his wand, the entire deluge careened into the dark army, crashing over them like a tidal wave.

"Good work!" Donna called out as she landed behind him.

Just then, the clouds above darkened. The darkness was so profound that it felt as if the sky had lost all shape. The throngs of enemies multiplied exponentially; where hundreds once stood, thousands now surged toward the dwindling allied forces. In the distance, a dozen more of those behemoths emerged from the shadows and raced over the masses toward them.

Jehu was surrounded by a frenzy of warrior minions, all attacking him with their swords. He used his magic and incredible skills to fend them off, but only for a limited time. Just as he dispatched five, a sixth stabbed him through the back, lifting his body up by the blade. Donna watched as Jehu's lifeless form was thrown back into the darkness, lost beneath the thousands of crushing feet.

"NO!" She raised her hands and wings, casting a shield wall that stretched wide across the field. The other wizards noticed her action and joined in, linking their own shield spells with hers. A massive wave of enemies slammed against the barrier, repeatedly attempting to break it down. Some of the wizards and gnomes had ascended the hillside and were swiftly taking down imps, as those creatures could fly right over the barrier.

Lord Brim came running across the field on the other side of the barrier. With his lava fists, he slammed into the behemoths, and their bodies crashed into each other. He wasn't doing much damage, but he was stalling them. Once they reached the barrier, it would come down.

"Watch, as Gallenor ends." The Dark Lady looked out across the darkness, trapping the last defenders.

Markus strained and said, "Steffen...please...let her go!"

Steffen, choked under the pressure of the dark spell cast over him, said, "I have. She is not my wife. I've accepted that."

The Dark Lady looked back annoyed. "What are you two babbling about?"

Markus ignored her. "No, your last memory. You have to....gah....you have to let her go."

Coming over quickly, The Dark Lady grabbed Markus by his face. "BE SILENT!"

Markus shook her hand off and tried to look fierce through the pain. "This isn't over."

She was about to say something when she lurched back and held her abdomen. "What...what is this?"

Steffen lifted the wand again and slammed the Pearl end into the ground. "I will never forget you." He slammed it once more. "But, I have to..." He slammed it again, "Let" and again, "you" and again, "GO!" This final slam broke the wand and shattered the Pearl. A small wave of light erupted from it. Though weak to Steffen or Markus, it was a tremendous explosion against Kellen, throwing him clear across the room.

The Dark Lady held herself. "What have you done!"

The drain from Markus into the core stopped, and he was freed of it. The chains binding him vanished. He confidently answered her, "Your only tie to reality was his persistence in holding onto the past. He kept you alive unwittingly by keeping Alieth alive in that wand. Just a small piece of her, hardly enough to really even be her. But enough for the Dark Pearl to keep you here."

She fell to her knees. "I'm so close... to true life."

Markus restrained himself from the pain that lingered within him. "You should never have existed. The Dark Pearl cannot create real life. Your existence had to come from something else. I realized that and finally understood how to destroy you. If you hadn't flaunted your Alieth visage in front of me, I would never have noticed the connection. I would never have recognized that it was intense love and determination to cling to that past that kept you alive. Steffen had to destroy his wand; it was the only way to fully break the connection and shatter you at last."

She grabbed the core and held it. "I can't die; I..." Suddenly, her body fractured as if it were pottery. Cracks formed all over. "I AM ALIETH! I AM THE DARKNESS! I CANNOT DIE!" She held her arms and writhed around like a marionette being tugged and yanked crassly. She screamed, cried, laughed. Her mind was withering away and her body continued to break. Shards of her evaporated one by one, dissolving her. The last piece of her was her head, mouth open in a scream as it plowed into the stone floor and breaking apart, spilling across the floor. The Dragonwand Core tumbled away. The last sound was a distant scream that faded as she finally met her end. Energy from the blue Dragonwand core surged back toward Steffen and Markus. Each instantly regained their strength.

Korvarsk fell back, holding his head. He hit the ground, groaning.

"How did you figure it out?" Steffen asked.

Markus summoned his Dragonwand and steadied himself with it. "I talked to the memory in your wand. It took me some time, but I realized you could never have defeated her, even when you thought you failed. She didn't truly exist, she was the shard of a terrible memory as much as the Alieth in your wand was the shard of your good memory. You had to let go of the Alieth in your wand, which would break the Pearl's hold on her form."

"About the Pearl..." Steffen looked up to see Kellen kneeling, holding the Dark Pearl. It emanated a strange purplish black mist surrounding him.

"It's mine. It needs a physical form. Take me, TAKE ME!" Kellens stared into it, smiling wickedly as the shadow surrounded him.

"Stop him!" Steffen yelled.

Markus held up his wand, but it wasn't his magic that stopped him. A blaze of fire shot out and hit Kellen, blowing him away from the Pearl and incinerating his body. When the fire stopped, there was nothing but a smoking carcass in the corner of the room. Korvarsk fell to his knees, after having done this.

"Korvarsk!" Markus ran for him, but was stopped when he held up his hand.

"No, it still has me! I can hear it in my head! It wants... ahhh... it wants to live. You have to destroy... STAY AWAY FROM IT!" His mind quickly vacillated between him and the darkness still tainting him. He threw his hand to the side and Markus was hit by a magic force and tumbled through the room.

Steffen clapped his hands and sent a shockwave at Korvarsk. The power knocked them over, Steffen mainly fell because he was still physically weak.

Markus got back up and had his wand ready to fight Korvarsk. But, Korvarsk shrieked, "No! Destroy the Pearl! Destroy it!"

"How?" Markus pleaded.

Korvarsk yelled, "Stay away from it!" He reared back and unleashed a volley of dark magic.

Steffen shoved Markus away and took the blast, skidding across the ground and finally hitting the back wall.

Korvarsk struggled harder, the darkness trying to consume his mind. He yelled incoherently as he clawed at his head. Finally, he screamed, "IT'S YOU! THE LIGHT! USE THE LIGHT, AND DESTROY THE DARK! IT IS SCARED OF YOU...AHHH!" He lost his moment of cohesion and his eyes went dark. The Pearl lifted and emitted magic into Korvarsk.

Markus pulled himself up with his Dragonwand and stood there for a moment. "How do I do this?" he whispered. The room was becoming filled with a hurricane of darkness. Misty blackness swirled around, touching everything. It lifted Korvarsk's body into the air and tinted his scaly skin black, creating a new champion, a new Dark Heart.

In the eye of the storm, Markus stood, trying to tap into the light again. Fear and anger would not help; they would only feed the

Pearl more darkness. Suddenly, a voice spoke in his ear—it was Tolen's. "Why did I give up everything to fight Hallond for a thousand years?" Markus closed his eyes, feeling that cold darkness inching closer, its screaming gales deafening. Tolen's voice echoed in his mind: "I fought the darkness not because I wanted to win the Dragon War, but because I loved my wife and child so much. They were innocent. I would give up my life to save theirs and all of Gallenor."

Markus asked, "How did I do it before? With the candles in Thendor? How did I direct the light so powerfully?"

Tolen's voice said, "Just think of that moment."

Markus recalled that moment. All his friends were in grave danger, and the girl he loved lay on the ground at his feet, inches from death. Markus looked up and said, "I was willing to do anything to stop the darkness, even if it meant sacrificing my own life."

"Yes. Evil is not destroyed by weapons or determination, it is defeated by the only thing it cannot truly understand, selfless love."

"I am not worthy of this. I am not strong enough."

Tolen answered, "It is not just you this day. It is all around you. So many have sacrificed everything to save this world and stop the darkness. Let their light shine... be the Heart of Light." Markus's mind filled with all that has happened since this battle started. Donna saved his life several times. The nation stood shoulder to shoulder, united to fight. King Brim led the gnomes into battle. It wasn't him they were fighting for, it was selfless love in their hearts to protect the innocent, the good, the hope of a better tomorrow. It was all their loved ones laying sick with the taint. The last image in Markus's mind was that of his final kiss with Crystal and how he knew he had to do anything he could to keep her safe.

"I understand," Markus whispered as the darkness finally enveloped him.

Suddenly, a brilliant light radiated from him. It spread outward and pushed the darkness away from the room. Once more, this wave of light emerged from him, and then again, and again. Wave upon wave of pure light exploded from with him.

The darkness within the Pearl lashed out. The black energy pushed back, forcing the light away. Markus did not stop; he only grew stronger as he continued. The waves of light emanating from him expanded and moved beyond the room, beyond the castle. Soon, the dark sky above dissolved away, revealing the sunshine again. The creatures nearest the castle screeched and screamed as they fled the pain.

While this onslaught of light continued, Markus lifted his Dragonwand and directed a light beam straight into the dark Pearl. Soon, the Pearl could not contain the power. The black energy was shoved within it, and the light slowly replaced the dark. Finally, the Dark Pearl rolled away, solid white. Markus hit the ground, breathing hard and holding his throat. He was spent, his eyes half shut, and his body resting on its side. He meekly whispered, "Is it over?"

As if to answer that, the Pearl blew up with a dark wave of energy shattering it into millions of pieces. A ball of pure light exploded in a massive wave that cracked the walls and foundation of this palace of darkness. With each inch it moved, the greater its power grew.

The warriors outside watched in utter astonishment when this storm of cloudy light rolled across the world. Every dark creature fleeing was nothing but smoke the moment it made contact with this wave. Even the massive, mighty behemoths were nothing but wisps of dissolving darkness that soon were gone. Those not of the darkness felt a bathing warmth across their bodies as this light pass them, a soothing of their souls like a strange, beautiful happiness was filling them. The dark sky was just a layer of gray clouds.

CHAPTER 7: AFTERMATH

DONNA slowly lowered her arms and wings, the magical barrier coming down. Before them, the terrible army was a black fog melting away on the breeze. Only the giant lava monster stood where their enemy once was. Sadly, those who had fallen in this battle were strewn across the field.

"Isss it over?" Vulshk asked.

Donna transformed into herself and took a cautious step forward. "I don't know."

Kellus pointed up. "Look, the skies."

Everyone watched as the clouds melted away. In a matter of seconds, a single hole of sky above the castle became a full blue sky from horizon to horizon. With this, the allied forces knew that it was truly over. Everyone began to cheer loudly, clapping hands and hugging one another. Even the gnomes were celebrating.

Crystal came running over to Donna. "Where is he?"

"Who?"

"Markus! Where is he?"

Kellus pointed at the castle. "Last I saw, he was heading for the..." They jumped when the castle had a massive crack form on its side. Spires and buttresses broke away and crashed to the ground.

"It's coming down!" Donna yelled.

Lord Brim raced to the castle and tried to hold it up with his huge arms. But it was flaking apart, and there was nothing left to keep it intact.

Korvarsk woke with his head aching and the room spinning. He quickly realized that the room was moving; it wasn't just him. The room tilted hard as the building cracked loudly and crumbled. Large portions of the ceiling broke free and crashed through the floor below, creating deep holes.

"Markus?" He stood by holding the wall but almost fell over as the room tilted more and he slid. "Markus!" He looked around and found Markus lying on the ground, now completely unconscious. He rushed over to his friend. "Markus! Come on! This place is gonna crash."

"Hey, kid!" Steffen yelled.

Korvarsk looked up. "Oh, good, you're still here. Okay, I can get us out here, I think. I don't feel strong right now."

"No, don't worry about me. Just get Markus away. And, don't leave this behind." Steffen tossed something at Korvarsk.

He caught it and found the blue Dragonwand core in his hand. "But, what about you?"

Steffen held onto the wall to keep from sliding. "I'm done. He's the Dragon now. Just, get him out."

"No, I can..." Korvarsk wanted to say more, but a massive chunk of the ceiling collapsed between him and Steffen.

Steffen yelled, "Get out of here before you both are squashed. I... have done what I came to do. GO!"

Holding out his hand, Korvarsk summoned his Dragonwand and quickly transformed. He picked up Markus while still holding onto that core. As the large piece of ceiling sank through the floor, he lifted off and flew out of the room. He glanced once back at Steffen, a pity in his dragon eyes.

Steffen, leaning against the wall, laughed. "I'm not going to lie here and die; I want to see the world before I go." As he stood in a window, he held on tightly as the top half of the castle swayed to the side. Behind him, the lava construct known as Lord Brim pulled back as the building started crumbling right above him. Now, it was just a matter of seconds before it all came crashing down.

Looking down at his arm, Steffen smiled with satisfaction. His skin was burned where he had been hit while protecting Markus. To anyone else, this would be a normal, albeit painful, burn. But he hadn't been bruised, cut, or burned in over three thousand years. His body was immune to injury. However, that was no longer the case; somehow, this experience altered that fate. "So, this is how I die? This is where it all ends. But what an end it is. She is gone forever, and the world is safe from her. My grandson is a wonderful, loving, kind, and smart boy with a great girl and a bright future ahead of him." The building tilted back and was almost ready to fall. He held tight and gulped. "Then... why am I scared?"

The castle finally crashed. The top fell over, crushing all that was below it. Steffen let go of the wall and fell freely in the air as the room was destroyed. Suddenly, something came blasting through the room, grabbed him, spewed a ball of fire to clear the way, and came out the other side. A Dragon carried him away from the castle, safe and secure.

"Markus?" Steffen asked.

Donna laughed and looked down at the man in her arms. "Did you think I'd let such a gorgeous hunk of man leave me after just one kiss?"

Steffen laughed a deep, hearty laugh.

CHAPTER 8: LIFE REKINDLED

A young nurse walked among the beds filling the Stillwater Community Center. Angela had hardly just graduated from the school of medicine when she was called to tend to the sick here. The doctors were all ill and the other nurses had slowly succumbed. She was alone in providing medical care. This illness defied all forms of aid. Her sole responsibility was to comfort the sick and transport the dead to the makeshift morgue outside of town. The normal morgue had long passed its capacity.

"Angela!" a boy called out from the side of the room as he clung to the windowsill.

"Torrik! I told you not to yell in this room." She hurried through the people, carefully navigating the limited walking space.

"You need to see this!" His voice was joyous.

Angela held no hope that what he saw would brighten the sorrow in her heart right now. Nothing brought pain to caregivers worse than being unable to truly provide care. She walked toward him not to see what flippant ounce of amusement he pointed to, but to take him away and tell him to stop making a nuisance of himself.

A gasp caught her ear, then a strange moan. The people in the room moved, some lifted their weak hands to their faces.

"What's happening?" She asked aloud.

The windows around the center light up with glorious sunlight, the first sunlight she has seen in days. Now she ran for the window, a spark of hope finally crackling in her gloomy heart.

Torrik gleefully said, "Sky! I see blue sky! See, see!"

She heard people breathing better and a few even speaking. That spark erupted into pure joy. "Oh, please, let this all be real." She held the boy next to her, both with glittery eyes at the beautiful skies above.

***

Kalvor, the obstinate Rakki guard who verbally assaulted Cranshk, walked through the mats laying out in the center of the Blue Forest Park, near the Grand Library of the Rakki. Almost every living soul in the forest lay on mats, slowly dying of this horrible disease. His superiors had left him there as one of the few guards not needed for the northern battle. Kellus clarified that Kalvor's attitude toward Shlan made him a risk during this critical mission.

At the edge of the mats was one that held a small, frail looking woman. Kalvor walked over and knelt down on the ground next to her. Taking up her weak hand, he held it against his chest. The only doctor left, who was currently traveling to the valley to see to the human farmers, had told him not to touch the sick, but he couldn't obey.

"My dear, please don't leave me. I love you. I can't lose you."

149

She slowly turned her head to him and weakly opened her eyes. "Why... are you... here? The war... "

He said, "Lord Kellus felt I would do better watching over the sick, protecting the forest. I... I can't lie to you now. Lord Kellus said he needed me to stay because I hate the Shlan so much, and he had ordered our armies to fight alongside them."

"Kal... I... I love you. You... need to resolve that... bitterness. Love... is better than hate." She closed her eyes.

Kalvor wept as he held her hand to his chest. "Please don't leave me. Oh, by the trees and library, I swear I'll learn to love everyone, as long as you are with me. Don't go. Please!" Her breathing was shallow, growing slower by the moment. He would hold her until her last breath and then try to figure out how to breathe without her.

A deeper breath came, then another. She opened her mouth to take in a greater breath. The grip on his hand by hers strengthened. The surrounding people all moved more, made noises, breathed clearly.

"Stana!" He called her name out with cautious joy.

A soft breeze rustled the leaves of the trees, and fresh light cut through the branches. Kalvor looked up at the blue skies singing with sunlight among the green foliage.

Stana, his wife, opened her eyes and smiled. "I feel better. So much better."

"Oh, Stana. I thought I had lost you." He could not contain his tears.

She said, "I will hold you to your promise."

***

Hlarsk sat in the palace courtroom at Thendor. For a moment, he looked around, amazed to be here, where the royal court would convene daily. Yet, right now, he was alone. The servants and courtiers were out fulfilling their duties. The skies had cleared, and reports of people quickly recovering from the taint had begun to trickle in. A cautious jubilation was growing among the population, but everyone was hesitant to celebrate too quickly since the armies had not yet returned.

Tears fell from his eyes looking down at a wand in his hands. This was just a wand belonging to someone he did not know. But, it looked a lot like his late wife's wand. The heartache at the idea he might have lost his son today was so strong he fought to drag air into his lungs.

Just then, a loud thump echoed outside. By now, he recognized what that sound meant. A dragon had just landed in the square. People outside were talking loudly, some even screaming. Hlarsk stood and rushed to the closed palace doors as quickly as possible. Without anyone's help, he pushed the doors open, which was no small feat. After letting them swing open, he paused and stared in complete disbelief. A dragon placed Markus on the ground, then transformed into Korvarsk. He helped Markus to his feet and led him to the stairs.

"I feel so lightheaded, but I think I'll be all right," Markus said.

Korvarsk gently led Markus to sit on the steps. "Are you sure?"

"Yes."

Hlarsk wanted to cry out and call his son by his name, but he couldn't muster the words. He fell to his knees and whispered, "Korvarsk."

That's all it took. Korvarsk looked up at his father. Running up the steps, he knelt and grabbed his father in a tight embrace. "Dad!"

"My boy... you are my boy. I know you." The smell, the feel, the sound of his voice, this was his son and Hlarsk had never felt such unmitigated joy in his life.

Korvarsk cried as he said, "I'm so sorry for what I did to you. I tried to stop myself. I tried to fight it, but I couldn't. I'm so sorry."

"You don't have to apologize. That horrible thing controlled you."

"Not anymore. She's dead, and the Pearl is gone. It's over, it's all over!" Korvarsk unleashed all the pent up sorrow and joy he held in as he returned here with Markus.

Hlarsk leaned on his son, never wishing to let go again. "I was so scared for you. When that awful woman ordered you to kill me, I was terrified that you would do it. That you would wake from whatever curse she had on you and live the rest of your life knowing that you murdered your own father."

Korvarsk sat back and looked his father in the eyes. "I would never do it. I couldn't. When she ordered me to do that, it enraged me. For only a short time, I could control myself, but only when I slept. I would wake in the middle of the night and have control. But, I couldn't do much; otherwise, I would wake the demon she placed in me."

"What are you saying?"

"I left you the notes, I gave you a path out of Shlan lands. I had to save you and hopefully give you what was needed to save the Shlan from a civil war."

"It was you?" Hlarsk whispered. How he escaped the Shlan lands had remained a mystery in his mind. "I never could figure out who saved me. I was happy I got away, but it seemed impossible. You were so clever."

"I found cleverness in desperation. I had to save you. I would not lose both parents to this evil. Not long after you left, I lost any amount of control. But, I knew that you were gone and safe. I'm so proud of you, Father. You came here and helped Markus and Steffen save Gallenor."

Hlarsk took his son in his arms again. "I did it all for you."

"Thank you for being so brave." Korvarsk leaned over and touched his forehead to his father's, a gesture of family between Shlan.

Hlarsk sat up and asked, "Why did you sign the notes 'T'?"

Korvarsk picked up the end of his tail. "Remember when I was very young, I would run around the house hiding. You would see my tail sticking out and say, 'There's my little tail.' You started calling me that."

"Yeah, I called you my little tail until you were three."

Korvarsk nodded. "That is the T, tail."

Hlarsk said, "But, I would never have thought of that. Did you really think I would put that together?"

Letting his tail go, Korvarsk shook his head. "No. I honestly didn't want you to know. If you knew I was able to help you, you might have tried to come and save me instead of following the path here that would keep you safe. I just wanted to sign it in a way that let me know I was really there, that I was still your son and wanted to save my father. It was a piece of my heart that she hadn't stolen from me yet. Besides, if anyone else saw it, they would have no idea what it meant."

"My little tail," Hlarsk whispered as he hugged his son. "I'm glad   you   are   here."

CHAPTER 9: DARKEST DAYS GIVE WAY TO LIGHT

"**WHERE'S** Korvarsk?" Steffen asked as he met Markus behind the family farmhouse.

Markus pulled off his father's beekeeping suit. "I'm not sure. He said something about dealing with his feelings right now."

Steffen let out a deep sigh. "I was concerned about your friend. He was forced to do some terrible things. It will take time for him to address all of that. But he's strong and has supportive friends."

"I told him to spend time with his father at the Shlan capital. I think working with the healers might help him feel better. It would also be great as they need people working so they can recover from the taint."

"Yeah, it's been a hard recovery for many places. But each day people are getting better. Speaking of that, how are your parents?"

Markus picked up the filled honey frames from his father's beehives and brought them inside the house. "They're doing well. The doctor says they should be back on their feet in a week. Not many people in the Valley died from the taint."

"They were fortunate. I heard the Port of Pearls suffered significant losses, as did Stillwater." Steffen walked with Markus into the kitchen, where Markus already had a knife in boiling water.

Pulling out the knife and setting the honeycomb frame on a bucket, he cut it into chunks, freeing it from the wooden frame. "Lord Flavian has sent me several messages about the situation. He's keeping everyone informed."

"He's a good man and a great leader," Steffen commented.

Markus smiled. "I think so, too."

Steffen picked up a small chunk of the cut comb and tasted it. "Oh, this is a nice crop. Where did you learn to do all that? Has your family always been honey farmers?"

"No. Dad got into it recently. Fortunately, Tolen spent about a century tending honey bees while he was teaching at the college, about three hundred years ago, I think."

Steffen said, "I'm glad I'm going to have time to learn all about what my boy did. I tried to keep up with him, but it isn't so easy at a distance."

Markus stopped his work and looked up at Steffen. "I'm glad you're here. I know you expected to die at her hands. Even at the end, you thought you would go down with that castle."

"I had decided long ago that if it came down to it, I would give up my life to protect this world. I thought that if she killed me, her link to this world would die as well and she would be gone. But..."

"That might have worked, but the Pearl would still be here, continuing to hurt people. We had to destroy her and the Pearl. If you had let her kill you, her power and corruption would have devastated this world. She would have vanished, but the Pearl would have corrupted someone like Kellen or Korvarsk."

Steffen nodded. "Yes. Tolen was always wiser than me, and I'm glad and fortunate that you garnered that from him. It saved us all."

"I have one question? Is the taint gone?" Markus asked.

"The taint is gone. The Pearl was the connection that gave the taint to this world. But, the darkness is still here."

"How? We destroyed the Dark Pearl."

Steffen said, "Think for a moment, did the Dark Pearl create the darkness?"

Markus paused and thought about that. "No. From what you told me, dark acts and absorbed darkness created the Dark Pearl."

"So, you see, darkness is the evil of this world born in the absence of good. Remember when you came to me seeking answers about the taint and darkness?"

"Yes, you said something about how that dark and light magic aren't real, that magic is just magic." Markus continued cutting up the honeycomb.

Steffen nodded while rubbing his bare arm. "I was correct, magic is just magic. Much as honey is just honey, it is what you do to it and with it that changes what it is. However, my experience with the Dark Heart at her castle gave me an insight I lacked."

Markus put the knife back into the simmering water to clean it off. "What do you mean?"

"I always thought dark and light were merely actions, outcomes of magic use. However, I had questions that were never answered. When the wicked magic users first crafted the Dark Pearl, they intended for it to absorb magic, but the magic used to create it was hateful, evil, and twisted. Thus, that is what the Pearl sought. It corrupted magic, distorting and altering it."

"Okay, so the pearl corrupted magic. Then, where did the light come from?"

Steffen paused to think for a moment. "I've reflected on that a lot since the battle. I always believed that my light was simply the opposite of her darkness. Just as I had unanswered questions about the darkness, the light felt foreign to me. When she tapped into my light and corrupted it to gain control over the Dragonwand core, I started to understand something. The light within me was altered magic, just like the dark magic."

Markus had a horrified look on his face. "What? Corrupted... light?"

"No. Not like that. You see, when I first discovered the dark pearl in the lost Ithorean city, it was already filled with terrible darkness and evil. This tattoo was given to me to imbue into me the light, created by five of the most powerful wizards of a bygone era. When I first contended against the power of this pearl, the spirits of those five gave me all their magic that I could finish the war. This created the light that I held in me and eventually passed down to you."

Markus asked, "Can you tell me more about that? I'd love to learn your history."

Steffen laughed and said, "It is a long story, for another time. For now, I want to focus on helping you understand the light. This magic sought out goodness, kindness, and especially love. Acts of purity could transform magic into something wonderful, just as darkness could corrupt it into something dreadful. I was infused with incredible light, rendering me untouchable by the darkness."

Markus sat down. "Why you? Why did you get the tattoo and the light?"

Steffen laughed. "It wasn't because I was some glorious, pure, righteous man. In fact, I was egotistical in my youth. When I sought out a witch to give me a spell, it was to enchant my body to look like this. I got that, and a tattoo. That witch was someone else, someone who set me on a path to fight darkness. They saw in me something I didn't realize was there."

"Three thousand years is a long path," Markus stated.

"Well, it wasn't supposed to take that long. No one can fully see the future, I hope you understand that. Magic cannot see past this moment. But, I was believed to defeat the Pearl the first time it rose and tried to conquer the world. However, I faltered... twice. The

Pearl had stolen the face of my beloved and that caused me to hesitate. The light magic in me was destined to defeat the darkness, that is what it was crafted for, and I failed to succeed. I think this is why it left me for you. It saw in you the kind of love that I once understood."

Markus shook his head. "No, the light came to me because you wanted to protect me. It was your love for me that connected the light in us. Mine grew stronger, but you never lost yours, not entirely."

Steffen laughed. "Boy, you really have Tolen's wisdom. Anyway, the light's mission has always been to defeat the darkness. That task is now accomplished. The Pearl is gone, so the spell that created the ultimate light has ended. That's why you can't tap into it like you could before."

Markus thought for a second. "What about the taint? If the Pearl only worked in corrupting magic, where did the taint come from, and how was it connected to the Pearl?"

"The taint was not a disease; otherwise, it could be cured by medicinal magic. No, it was merely the corrupting of the magic within a person."

"But, it tainted non-wizards."

Steffen shook his head. "Magic is within everyone. Most are so weak they will never tap into it, but strong ones become wizards."

"I... I didn't know that."

"I learned that from the fairies. Magic has spread across all peoples through genetics. Some, like the Shlan, have very little among their genes, so only a few can become wizards. Others, like humans, have a deep pool of magical genes; thus, most wizards are human." Steffen picked up another chunk of the honeycomb.

Markus had a profound "ah-ha" look on his face. "It makes sense now."

"What?" Steffen seemed amused by this.

"You mentioned that the Dark Lady drew power from spreading the taint. I couldn't grasp that; it didn't seem to make sense. However, if corrupted magic nourished the Pearl, then the taint would serve as a pure source of dark power for the Pearl. It all makes sense now."

"Precisely." Steffen shoved a large chunk of honey-filled comb in his mouth and chewed it thoughtfully.

Markus took the hot knife out and started cutting again. "There is one more thing. What happened to your tattoo?"

Steffen gazed at his arm. "The tattoo was a way to connect with the light magic within me. It weakened when the magic passed to you. It protected me, more than I care to admit. The spell of that tattoo defended me even in those final moments; her drain should have killed me, but it didn't. However, the tattoo is finally expended and gone forever. The magic of the ancients has departed, and I am no longer invulnerable. In fact, I have returned to what I was before the tattoo: a fairly weak wizard."

They both looked up when the unmistakable sound of wings flapping grew loud, followed by a thud. A Dragon had just arrived.

"Oooh, my girl's here," Steffen smiled.

Markus laughed. "You really do like her."

"I love that girl. She is so... so... full of life."

Donna knocked and walked in at the same time. "Anyone home!"

Markus was about to greet her, but Steffen beat him to it. He ran over and grabbed her in his arms, spun around once, and then kissed her with gusto. Finally coming up for air, he said, "Are you looking for me?"

She got down from his grip and unashamedly ran her hand down his muscular bare chest, "No, but I'll never turn that down."

Markus came over. "Hello, I'm here too."

Donna retorted, "Oh, you and Crystal are just as bad."

"True." Markus admitted, knowing just how mushy they acted around each other regardless of who was nearby.

Donna went around him. "Oh, look. You're cutting honeycomb. Can I have some?" She already had a chunk of the comb in her hand.

"Sure." Markus was shaking his head with a wry chuckle.

Steffen asked, "What brings you out here? I thought you were helping at the Port of Pearls."

She talked around a mouthful. "I was. I had to drop Lord Flavian off at the capital. I came across Treb who had something for Markus. I said I'd bring it here on my way back to the port."

"What is it?" Markus asked.

She pulled out the long box with the necklace. "He said something... what was it... "Oh", he said, "Tell that boy he's got a responsibility to take care of' whatever that means."

Markus took the box and spent a moment just staring at it.

Steffen finally asked, "What is it?"

Markus said, "It's something I must do before anything else goes wrong."

"What?" Donna asked.

Markus looked up and said, "I'll tell you guys later. Donna, head back to the port and help out, Steffen, could you lend a hand here in the valley?"

"Sure."

"Great. I have to go to the Blue Forests soon." Markus returned to the honey comb.

***

Gentle ocean waves lapped at the coastline around the Port of Pearls. The waters were still littered with the burnt debris from the dragon's attack. The docks were quiet right now; it was early, and the cleanup crews were not yet at work. Normally, before the attack, the docks would already be bustling with all sorts of activity, but not today.

In the water, standing alone, was a small platform that had once been the end of a dock. It was broken and burned, yet still flat. The length that had led back to the land was gone, its shattered remains washed out to sea days ago. Yet, a lone figure sat on this, his feet dangling over the edge. He looked down into the surface of the ocean and watched the ripples from each teardrop falling in. Korvarsk dipped his toes into the water and wiggled them, remembering the last time he had sat here. Sh'arna was beside him, gushing about how much she wanted to see the Shlan homelands.

Listening to the memory of her sweet voice stirred a rage in his belly. He summoned the Dragonwand and held it in his hand for a moment before pitching it into the waters, watching it splash and sink. However, not too far down, that beautiful white staff vanished. With a single thought, he summoned the Dragonwand again, and it was in his hands.

"I hate this damn wand. I never wanted to be a Dragon," he muttered, staring morosely at the staff.

Then, he noticed something new. Another person's reflection was in the water, standing beside his seated reflection. Looking to his right, he found that same person standing there. She was a tall, strong-looking woman with white and gold wizard robes. She slowly sat next to him. "Why did you try to throw it away?" she asked.

Korvarsk's eyes were wide. "How did you get out here? I had to fly to get to this. The docks are destroyed... no thanks to me."

She smiled and touched the wand. "I'm not sitting next to you; I'm in your hands."

He looked down and felt the wand; it was slightly warm and emitting magic. "Oh, you're an imbued memory?"

"Yes. Before all the Dragons abandoned our titles and sent the cores away for safe keeping, we placed our essence in them to help those who inherited them. I can answer questions and guide you."

"Like Tolen guides Markus?"

She nodded, "Yes, Tolen would have done the same. I have been watching you, Korvarsk. I am the Liliana, the Dragon of Wind, your title as a Dragon."

"I know. I've already seen some of your memories and experiences."

"I have witnessed some of your actions since you obtained the wand. I have observed the terrible things that the Heart of Darkness caused through you. I have also seen the deep regret and pain you have experienced over the past weeks since you regained your mind."

Korvarsk gazed at the water, his eyes filled with sorrow and his posture bent. "It's not just pain; it's unbearable agony. I've seen myself commit horrible acts, killing people both here and in my own lands."

"You do understand that it was not you who did this?"

"I know, Markus said that; my father has said it; even Crystal told me. I don't care! They don't understand what it's like! They never had their hands stained with the blood of innocent victims! They never had to watch children burn alive before their eyes! They..." His rant cut off as he succumbed to tears, "they don't know what it's like."

"No, they don't know what you've been through, just as you can't know what they've experienced. However, they are correct; the truth is that the person behind all that evil was not you."

He wiped his eyes and quietly said, "I can't make the agony go away."

She smiled at his reflection. "That's good."

"What? What good is agony?"

"No, not the pain itself, but the understanding of right and wrong. Your heart aches for the loss and tragedy. You have been entrusted with an incredible responsibility, the power and authority of a Dragon. Without a heart full of compassion and wisdom, such power would be wasted and pose great danger. You know right from wrong."

"That doesn't make it better," Korvarsk said. "Right where you're sitting, a girl sat beside me. She was full of life and hope. She had dreams. I promised her that I would take her to her homeland one day and show her the place where her people once ruled a mighty empire. She lived a life of servitude and suffering. On the day she was freed from that, when her life was about to improve, I killed her, her sister, her father, her friends, everyone."

"You did not kill her," she firmly stated.

"I might as well have."

After a long pause in deep thought, she said, "One of the greatest powers evil has in this world is making good people feel guilty for what they cannot control. She used you against your will and now you are still giving her power by letting your grief overtake your life. Instead of letting your experiences bury you in guilt and sorrow, learn from them."

"Learn from them?"

"You have the unique experience of seeing through the eyes of evil. You understand how deep depravity can go. Not even Tolen the Wise ventured into the darkness like you. Instead of letting it continue to consume and destroy you, digest it, understand it, and grow wiser from it. Allow the knowledge from it to guide you in making this world a better place. Don't let that poor girl, or anyone else, die in vain; let their deaths impart knowledge and wisdom so you can combat that evil when it arises again."

Korvarsk sat up a bit straighter. "I never considered it like that. I want the memories to vanish, to have never occurred. I suppose that isn't possible. But, I can turn them into a lesson for others."

"Yes. History repeated itself three times, use your wisdom to prevent a fourth. Evil didn't die in the Dark Pearl; it still resides in this world. You can fight it."

Korvarsk almost smiled. "I will. For Sh'arna's sake and all those who died from the Dark Lady's corruption, I will stand against the darkness."

With a smile, this strong woman nodded to him. "The greatest teacher is experience. Never waste a true experience."

Korvarsk looked out and saw a ship coming in to the port. There was already a temporary dock so that operations could resume. "I can do this, I can make this world better."

"Good."

He sat there, his brief happiness fading softly as he became lost in those thoughts again. "Will it make the pain go away?"

"What?"

"Using this knowledge, growing from the experience, all you've said. Will it ever make the pain go away?"

She leaned over and wrapped an arm around him. "No, that will always be a part of your heart. But it will get easier as you move forward. Trust me, all the Dragons have faced times that caused us great pain which we've had to deal with. For now, allow yourself to be sad, but don't lose yourself in the sorrow. Don't dwell on what was lost; remember what has been saved and what can be new. Show the world the kind of love that can fight the evil you've experienced. Fill your heart with great memories of new experiences filled with joy, love, and happiness. In time, those fresh, positive memories will give you the strength to move on from this and feel whole again."

"I will try."

She smiled with a motherly warmth, "I will always be here with you. Your friends and family will stand beside you. Don't sit by yourself in sorrow. Reach out to them when the darkness in your mind comes back to haunt you."

For the first time, Korvarsk honestly wept. The woman, who was indeed just in his mind from the Dragonwand, vanished. Behind him, the workers came to continue cleaning the damage gathered. They all knew who this was, but they were not afraid of him anymore. They could hear him crying and all stood in silence, awed by the sight of a Dragon's tears.

***

Markus walked through the Blue Forest city of the Rakki. People stopped and stared, and more than one approached him and wanted to meet him. He didn't even have his Dragonwand with him; he was dressed in regular wizard robes, yet they recognized him.

"My Lord Dragon," a guard approached and bowed to him, "Lord Kellus is away at the capital right now."

Markus did his best not to roll his eyes. "I know, five other guards have informed me of that fact already. I'm not here to see Lord Kellus, this is a personal visit."

The guard stood straighter. "Would you need an escort?"

"I know the way, and I don't need protection. But, thank you for the offer." He kindly bowed out of this and went on his way, going down paths that did not have guards on them that he could see.

He approached the medical ward where he first met Crystal. A dozen medical wizards were working around it, not all Rakki. They became alert and hushed when Markus approached.

"My Lord Dragon. Um, what...sorry to sound rude, but what are you doing here?" an older medical wizard asked.

Markus looked around. "I'm here to see Crystal."

"Crystal, oh, she is down with the others. This is only for doctors up here."

"Thank you." He walked around and down another path until he reached an area where the Rakki archers trained. The area was a large, flat part of the cleared forest. Unfortunately, right now, it was littered with cots and blankets where people were being treated.

Coming into this area, he stepped around people, acknowledged a dozen other greetings, and headed directly for the girl he had been searching for. Crystal was treating a few elderly using a potion.

"That's right, drink it all up. You'll feel a lot better quickly." She gingerly tipped the vial up for the old Rakki man.

After wiping his mouth, he said, "I already feel so much better; I just need to regain my strength."

"You'll recover soon, I'm sure."

The man's eyes widened as he attempted to sit up. "My Lord Dragon!" This garnered a lot of attention from those around them.

Markus knelt and put a hand on the man's chest to guide him back down. "Please, don't strain yourself."

"Thank you, my Lord. Your wonderful girlfriend has been extremely kind to all of us." The people of this city were well aware of the relationship between Markus and Crystal, and they took great pride in it.

Crystal handed the man a book. "You keep reading, and I'll see what the Lord Dragon is here about." Her teasing tone made the old man smile and Markus smirk.

She got up with Markus and they walked away. Markus asked, "How goes the recovery?"

"Same as the rest of Gallenor. It's been two weeks since the incident, but people are still recovering. This is much worse than the taint in Thendor."

"I know. I suspect the taint intensified when she spread that dark storm over the land. But, the taint itself is gone now."

"Yes," Crystal said with joy. "They're all improving rapidly. We've already discharged several of them. It shouldn't be long now. How are things in the Valley?"

Markus smiled. "Good. Those old farmers should be up and plowing in no time. I've had to tend to my parents' honey bees several times. Someone needs to teach those bugs respect, they shouldn't sting the Lord Dragon."

Crystal scoffed, "What, did they deflate some of that ego?"

"Ha ha," Markus retorted.

Crystal went over to a cart with a selection of prepared potions. "What are you doing here? Just checking on the progress?"

"No. I have a special reason for being here. First, how are your parents?"

Crystal stopped moving the bottles around. "They are a lot better, but still have some recovering. The taint hurts wizards differently than non-wizards. Also, Rema had to blast them pretty hard to keep them from hurting others. But, even after all that, they'll be fine."

"Are they awake? Can I speak to them?" Markus asked.

Crystal frowned at him. "Yeah, they're awake. I nearly tied my dad to his bed to stop him from trying to get up and help. He needs rest. Why?"

"I'll tell you in a moment. Where are they?"

She had a curious, almost distrustful look in her eyes. "Over there, in that tent with the other recovering wizards."

He leaned over and kissed her on the cheek. "Meet me over by the Library in ten minutes."

"Why?"

"I'll let you know when I arrive." He hurried away to dodge further inquiries.

Markus stepped around more cots and beds and finally entered the tent with the wizards. There were only six beds in here with people lying in them.

A single young nurse sat near the entrance, preparing potion bottles. She stood quickly. "Lord Dragon!"

At that, the other wizards in their beds tried to sit up. Markus held out his hands. "Please, stay down. I'm not here as the Lord Dragon today. Please, I just need to speak with Fiona and Shio."

"Oh, uh, Doctor Fiona and Doctor Shio are back there." She kindly directed him to the last two beds in the room.

Markus walked through, hoping no one would notice the loud thumping in his chest. The color of his complexion deepened, and he gulped more than once. Finally, he stood before them, a bed on either side of him. "Fiona... Shio?"

"Markus? What's wrong?" Fiona asked.

He cleared his throat and fidgeted a few times, "Um, I... uh... I need your permission."

Crystal patiently waited before the massive doors that led into the Rakki Library. She was muttering to herself with irritation.

"I have a lot of work to do. I don't care if he's the Lord Dragon." She paced harder and harder as she kept saying this.

Finally, Markus came down the curved path, walking a bit slower than she expected. His look was worrisome.

"Markus? Is something wrong?"

He approached and stood before her, quiet for a moment as if he were contemplating something. "No... nothing's wrong."

"What did you have to talk to my parents for? Are they all right?"

"They're fine, perfectly fine."

"Good?" She frowned at him. "Then, why do you look like you're about to pass out?"

He gulped and looked up from her to those doors. "Do you remember how we met?"

"Of course. I remember when you and Treb brought Kiin into the medical ward after that imp attack. You were the first human wizard I had ever met. I also remember that you were a giant flirt."

Markus smiled in humor. "It's hard not to flirt when such a pretty girl is paying attention to me."

"You're still a flirt," she muttered.

"I remember that day well. I saw you and was captivated. You were the prettiest, smartest, and most fascinating person I had ever met. I wanted to get lost in those crystal blue eyes, listen to all that knowledge you had, and hold you close when you hurt. I remember when you brought me to this library to show me the magic books you learned from."

Crystal laughed. "I remember you scaring the librarian half to death."

Markus stepped closer. "From the first day I met you, I wanted to be with you every single day after that. I was so happy when you chose to join me on my journey to find the Dragonwand. I knew Treb was furious, partly because you defied him, but mostly because I was flirting with you. I couldn't help myself. Even now, it's hard to imagine spending a day apart from you. You give my life more meaning than the Dragonwand or all the accolades combined. I'm nothing without you."

"What are you saying?"

Markus slowly pulled out a nice box. "The reason I went to see your parents was to ask permission. I know it isn't a Rakki custom but a human custom."

"Permission?"

"Your father said yes, and I hope you do too." He opened the box, revealing the engagement necklace. "Crystal, will you be my wife?"

Crystal was left speechless. She gently took the necklace and examined it. Her eyes met his softly, mistiness swelling in them. Finally, she exclaimed, "Yes. Oh, yes!" Leaping onto him, her arms wrapped around his neck with the necklace still clutched in her hands. She hugged him so tightly that they nearly toppled over.

Separating their embrace momentarily, Markus placed the necklace around her neck. He fastened it behind her and stood back, his hands holding hers. "You're so beautiful."

She closed the space between them and kissed him. What began as a short peck quickly turned into a passion-filled embrace.

CHAPTER 10: A NEW KING

MARKUS stood before a gathering of people in the town square of Thendor. To his right stood Donna and Korvarsk, who made up the rest of the current Dragon Council. Kellus was nearby with Kiin and Treb. Norl and the race representatives stood with Lord Flavian and his family. In the front row of people, seated on the ground, were scribes ready to record everything said and done here.

Markus spoke into a small magic sphere being emitted by the top of his Dragonwand. "It has been one month since the last battle in the northern wastelands. Before that time, a taint spread throughout Gallenor, claiming many lives, but ceased when the darkness was defeated. I, the Lord Dragon, along with the other members of the new Dragon Council, will travel to each city to honor the fallen from those cities and to answer questions. I want to make it clear now, and each time any Dragon speaks at a memorial, that no life lost is any less precious than another. Today, I want to acknowledge the loss of a great man and leader of Gallenor. Lord Shashla'yar of the Shlan fell in combat, giving his life to defend another. Lord Kellus of the Rakki was spared death thanks to the noble actions of Lord Shashla'yar. His name will never be forgotten, and his statue will be erected here in Thendor to remind us of a man who understood honor better than many I have ever known. Please, step forward, Lady Y'alla and Lady Byhala'yar."

Two women stepped up from the Shlan delegation. One was older than the other, each were painted in sorrow, but kept their regal bearing. They ascended the steps and stood before Markus.

Markus first looked down at the older woman. "Lady Y'alla, your husband was a fine man who honored his ancestors as much as he honored his people." He then turned to the girl beside her. "Lady Byhala'yar, your father had much love in his heart. He often questioned his honor, but that only proved he possessed honor. He understood humility, and I can only hope to demonstrate such humility in my journey through life. He will be greatly missed." The girl tried to speak but could only manage soft sobs. Markus stepped back and bowed to Lord Kellus.

Kellus stepped forward, followed by Treb. Treb handed Kellus a beautiful sword and then stepped back. Kellus presented the sword. "Byhala'yar, your father saved my life. I cannot repay what he has done for me and my people. He..." he paused to collect himself. "He was a great man and a credit to your people. He always sought peace between our races. Though we have both indulged our bigoted past, he rose above it. I would like to present his sword to you. I took it from where he fell and used it to cut down many enemies. The sword of the King of the Shlan in the hands of the King of the Rakkiis truly time to recognize the peace we will hopefully share from now on."

The girl took the sword and held it close to her. Weeping over it, Lord Kellus stepped up and held her momentarily. Once he returned to his place beside Markus, Lord Norl came forward.

Norl held up a parchment. "Lady Byhala'yar, according to Shlan tradition, your father's title will pass to you. However, since you are only fourteen, it is not appropriate to assign you such responsibility. Therefore, we will ask your mother to take his place until you are ready."

Y'alla bowed. "I accept and will guide my daughter along her journey to assuming her rightful place on the throne."

Norl slowly lowered the parchment. "There is one more issue at hand. According to the laws of Gallenor, a new provincial governor can be established by a council, but a new Race Lord cannot. That authority can only be granted by a sitting king. Currently, the line of King Anthony is broken. The last claim to the throne belonged to the former Baron Thorne, who is now disgraced and facing trial for treason." He paused and stepped back.

The crowds grew in murmurs and a few outright questions. Markus stood before them once more. "The laws of Gallenor are ancient. Some of our most ancient laws are around the establishment of the royal family. Few know that the last Merlin placed the original Royal Family before he left Gallenor. The law allows Merlin or his Heir to establish a new King. I am the heir of Merlin, but I am not going to establish a new King, for the same Merlin who established the original line of King Anthony happens to be with us today." Markus stood back and waited.

Steffen stepped out of the palace, dressed in far less regal attire than the others. He held a scroll in his hand and stood before the crowd. "Hello. It has been a long time since I was here, in this city, to establish leadership for this land. It was only after great strife and war that I crowned a king before, and once again I find myself facing a nation that has endured much strife and war. However, it is my hope to usher in a new dawn of peace and justice by naming a king to the throne." He walked over to Lord Flavian and held out a scroll. "On this day, the people of Gallenor need leadership and guidance. They require a cool head and rational clarity. I have watched in astonishment as you quickly and expertly asserted these qualities to bring stability to a chaotic situation. More importantly, your actions were always for the betterment of this nation and its people. Not once did you put your own personal feelings or ambitions before the welfare of Gallenor. You have demonstrated the qualities of a king. Unless there are other challengers to my authority and choice, I name you, King Flavian the First, Ruler of the land of Gallenor."

Markus was now on, he stepped up. "As leader of the Dragon council and adviser to the council of representatives, I ask if any present challenge this decision? Let your voice be heard or remain silent forever on the matter of kingship." Everyone waited and no one spoke.

Steffen unrolled the scroll and extended it. Donna approached with a quill and ink. As Lord Flavian affixed his signature to the scroll, Steffen proclaimed, "By your signature, you obligate yourself to uphold the rule of law in the land, to abide by the council of representatives, and to defend Gallenor against its enemies both without and within. This binding agreement establishes your right to rule as the ultimate word and authority within the laws of the land. You will always honor and defend the Constitutional Concordat, which was signed in good faith by all races of Gallenor, establishing equality and due representation in the court of the Palace of Thendor."

Lord Norl stepped forward holding a small box containing the magical sealing wax. He lifted it as Trivian raised a large signet ring. Flavian placed the ring on his finger. Norl dripped a small amount of the wax next to his signature. Flavian pressed his ring into the wax and then pulled it away. The magical wax settled into the paper, binding Lord Flavian's symbol to the agreement he had just signed.

Up until this point, everything had already been rehearsed. Markus spoke again and it was news for Flavian. Markus said through his Dragonwand so everyone could hear, "The crown of the throne of Gallenor has held on it the symbol of the house of King Anthony and his ancestors for over a thousand years. The fall and disgrace of that family has left the crown unsuitable to represent the throne under new kingship. However, a new crown has been fashioned that will represent the family of King Flavian from here and through many generations. This crown is special as it was constructed not by the hands of any of the races here, but by the hands of another race." He stepped back.

From within the palace stepped out a small contingent of Gnomes. Lord Brim, the ancient Gnome lord from the volcano, was at this group's head. Beside the Gnome King, four gnomes held a the corners of a single pillow with the crown. The crown glimmered with silver and gold. All over it were placed the most exquisite gems anyone had ever seen. The crowds were awash with astonishment, other than a small handful, none had seen a gnome before.

Lord Brim spoke, and his voice resonated through the stone of the ground and walls for all to hear. "King Flavian, ruler of the races of the land known as Gallenor, you showed me and my kind respect and kindness in our darkest hour. You aided the Lord Dragon in bringing us back from the brink and infused hope into my life. We, the Gnomes, honor and acknowledge the kingship of Flavian the First. We wish to reenter the world and be allies and friends with our neighbors of Gallenor. To solidify this bond, we crafted you this crown. Forged in the lava of my northern throne, this crown is magical and will help you better understand all peoples. No language will be foreign to your ears while you wear this crown. Please, kneel.

Flavian came down to his knee and held out his hands. The crown was given to him, and he handed it to Markus, who properly handed it to Steffen. Flavian stood, and returned to his knees, facing the crowds.

Steffen held the crown over him. "As the last Merlin, leader of magic, co-author of the original Constitutional Concordat, and eldest living resident of Gallenor, I crown you King Flavian the First, Lord of Thendor, Race Lord of the Humans, and King over all of Gallenor." With that, he placed the crown on Flavian's head. Finally, he yelled, "Long live the king!" The gathered civilians and officials broke into applause and jubilation.

Crowned and standing, King Flavian stepped up where Markus had been. He waited until the crowds grew silent. Finally, he had their attention. "I am not a man for long speeches. I am overwhelmed by this gesture and will do everything I can to be worthy of the honor bestowed upon me this day. I invite each of the Race estates to come to me over the next few weeks, so that we can converse, and I can better understand your needs and desires. I welcome the insights and guidance from the council of representatives and the council of the Dragons. A wise man once said that we are united people. The reason we overcame darkness and finally triumphed in the war wasn't due to sheer strength alone, but because we were not truly divided. Standing together is how we will preserve the greatness of our nation." Applause and cheers followed his words. Once that subsided, he turned to the Shlan. "As my first official decree, I, King Flavian the First, officially recognize the leadership of Y'alla of the Shlan. I also acknowledge the future leader of the Shlan, Lady Byhala'yar. If there is anything I can do to support either of you during your transition into power, please do not hesitate to ask."

Both Shlan royals bowed before Flavian. Lady Byhala'yar said, "Long live the king!"

The crowd cheered as King Flavian approached and personally spoke to Y'alla and Byhala'yar. Markus and the others stepped back inside, ready for all the following questions and discussions. Transitioning into new authority was never easy. But, with the ancient wisdom of Markus and the ancient knowledge of Steffen, it wouldn't be so hard.

***

King Flavian stood before a small gathering in the middle of the college of wizardry. He was dressed in the finest royal attire as he officiated this event.

"It is with great pride and honor that I declare you man and wife, you may kiss the bride."

Donna pulled Steffen closer and gave him a passionate kiss. Those present applauded, and a few even chuckled. Once they finished kissing, which lasted a bit longer than tradition dictates, they stood with the king behind them. A small band played music as the couple walked back down the aisle as husband and wife.

A short while later, everyone gathered in the reception hall. Most of the attendees were other college instructors and students.

Markus and his parents, Crystal and her parents, Kiin and Treb, Korvarsk and Hlarsk, and, of course, the royal family were all present for this event.

"I think it suits you," Markus said.

King Flavian fixed the crown on his head. "I was hesitant to accept the throne when you and Steffen approached me about this. I still don't think I'm worthy of the title, but I'm doing my best."

Markus shook his head. "You're doing great. Trust me, Tolen lived through the entire line of King Anthony's family, I've seen many kings and queens of Gallenor. You're doing a great job already."

"There is so much to do."

Markus took a sip of his drink and cleared his throat. He was delaying what he had to say. "I do have one issue that hasn't been addressed yet."

Flavian smiled as he casually said, "the fact that my son cannot succeed me."

Markus was surprised. "Oh, you know."

"Yes, I have been reading all of the ancient and obscure laws that govern Gallenor. The law that prohibits a wizard from beecoming king is not well known, as none of the line of Anthony Anthony's lineage were ever wizards. a wizard. However, Trivian is a wizard, which creates a problem."

"Does Trivian know?" Markus asked

185

Flavian nodded. "He does, and he understands. The wisdom behind that law still makes sense. I also understand that I'm responsible for producing an heir to take my place when the time comes. My wife and I are young enough still to expand our family. Don't worry about us."

Markus was uncomfortable with the conversation. "Good, good. Now, where is Steffen and Donna?"

"They just came back in. Over there." Flavian pointed as he stood. "And I shall speak with them before I have to go. The court has a meeting with the reconstruction teams later this afternoon. If you would excuse me." Flavian bowed out and headed for the couple meeting everyone.

Markus drank the last of his beverage and saw a couple seated in the back. He got up and headed through the small crowd. At a table in the corner sat Treb, Kiin, and Korvarsk. Kiin was rocking their baby in her arms as they conversed.

Korvarsk was speaking to them. "In my second year here, I had a terrible history instructor who always reminded me that the Shlan rejected any wizards in their lands for four centuries after the war. Overall, though, this place was a positive experience."

"What's the big discussion?" Markus approached, taking a moment to smile at the baby in Kiin's arms.

Treb answered, "Korvarsk is just telling us about school here. This is only my second or third time ever being here."

Markus took a seat and noticed what each was wearing. "I see you both have translation pendants."

Kiin held up hers. "Yeah, your friend made one for each of us."

Korvarsk gave a knowing nod to Markus. "The leader of the Dragon Council has tasked me with helping to revive and educate Gallenor about ancient magic. I learned a great deal about it before I acquired the Dragonwand, and I recently discovered that the Dragon before me was a master of ancient magic techniques."

Markus returned the nod with a touch of snark. "As I understand it, each Dragonwand Core picks a person who fits well to the qualities of the person before. So to extend the former Dragon's good work and efforts. Thus it would make sense that your core chose you, as you already had an interest in ancient magic, which will only grow as you learn from your predecessor's wisdom and experiences."

Treb frowned. "I still don't get it. Both of you are Dragons, and so is Donna. She is the eldest of the group, Korvarsk is older than you, and yet you're the leader. That doesn't make sense. Isn't Korvarsk also your wizard mentor?"

Markus said, "The title and duty of leader falls to the owner of the Fire Dragon's wand, as the Fire Dragon was the council leader. He was the wisest Dragon, and with Tolen in my head, that wisdom gives me the aid I need to be the leader. Though, I don't throw around my weight as a leader often, I respect these two and their greater experience in this life."

Korvarsk added, "I'm not his mentor... anymore."

Kiin cocked her head. "What? But you went through the ritual, right? You are his master and Markus is your apprentice."

Markus answered, "He was my master, briefly. However, after recent events, he resigned as my master."

"Why?" Treb asked.

Korvarsk explained, "Gaining a Dragonwand made me realize just how much knowledge and wisdom is embedded in them. I was unable to teach Markus anything new. Simply teaching him about politics in Gallenor was hardly the work of a master wizard. I can teach him that without being his mentor."

"So, you don't have a master?" Kiin asked, shifting the baby from arm to arm.

"I have one. Steffen has agreed to be my wizard master. Unlike anyone else in Gallenor, he can teach me about magic in ways that I can't learn from this Dragonwand. He can also help me learn more about being a Dragon and using this wand; it was his at one time, after all."

Korvarsk laughed. "Don't think that I'm upset about this. Do you know how nervous I was about calling myself the master of The Lord Dragon of Gallenor? I felt like a fraud. Even though we both understood that I couldn't teach him anything about magic, I had this concern in me all the time about guiding him in the ways of magic as my own master had. I'm happy to just be his friend and fellow member of the Dragon council."

"Speaking of the Dragons," Treb said, "have you found someone for that blue core? And, what about the others?"

Markus shook his head. "I have not. And I won't. The core will select the rightful owner in time. I cannot do that. As for the others, they will reveal themselves in due time. Steffen is the only one who knows where they would be, and he won't say. I guess it makes sense. They are extremely powerful and could attract some very bad attention if someone tried to steal them. They will remain where they have been until such a time as they select owners."

Korvarsk said, "I suspect they will select soon. The council is reforming and knowing the ancient magic of those cores, they will want to be held again."

"There are five more, right?" Treb asked.

Markus shook his head. "Four. Not counting the blue core, there are four others. The total number of Dragons on the council will be eight."

"Eight? But, at the citadel there were nine seats," Kiin said.

"True. But, there were only ever eight real Dragons. The ninth was a false Dragon, created using the Dark Pearl. Hallond was never a real Dragon. He fooled them for a long time."

Korvarsk softly said, "Let's talk about happier things. The Dark Pearl still gives me chills to think about."

Markus smiled and looked at Treb. "Have you two decided on a name for the baby? Her naming day will be this week." He nodded toward the sleepy baby cuddled up against Kiin.

Treb arched an eyebrow. "You will find out then."

Kiin said, "I am leaning toward Lilly since her fur is so white."

Treb grunted, "So much for keeping it a secret."

Korvarsk smiled. "Lilly is beautiful. I do find it interesting that her fur is so white. I don't think I've seen a Rakki quite that color."

Kiin rocked the baby a bit. "I've never seen one either. No one can figure it out. But, she's beautiful."

"She's very beautiful," Markus said.

"Oh, look, Donna and Steffen are coming this way," Treb said.

Markus replied, "You don't sound too pleased."

"I'm happy for them, it's just they are so mushy it's kinda sickening."

Kiin added, "And you're jealous."

"Me! Jealous! What?" Treb blurted.

Kiin smiled at him. "You loved the way she fawned over your muscles, pinched your butt, and flirted with you. Now, she has another man to do all that to, and you miss the attention."

"I did not like how she pinched me inappropriately, and I hardly noticed how she fawned over my..." He saw that mischievous

190

look in Kiin's eyes and heard the way Markus was snorting. "I'm not fooling anyone, am I?"

Kiin and Markus both said, "Nope."

"Okay, so maybe I do miss it. I mean, what man wouldn't like girls flirting with him?"

Kiin leaned over and handed him their baby. "You have two girls who love and adore you, that is all that should matter."

Treb's embarrassed face melted as he looked at his daughter. "Yeah, I've got a lot of love right here from the both of you. Who could ever need anything more?"

Markus stood. "I think I'll leave you before this gets any mushier. And, I see my girlfriend sitting with both her parents and mine, which can only mean trouble. So, if you would excuse me." He left them to their conversation.

Markus cautiously approached the table with his family and soon-to-be in-laws. They hardly noticed him approach.

"I don't think that's so wise. I know we have the space for everyone, but we just don't have the amenities." Thomas answered something his wife said.

"But, it's his home," Margaret protested.

Markus sat down. "What's the big discussion?"

Crystal took his hand and answered. "We're just talking about where to hold the wedding."

Markus slunk back. "Oh, that again."

Crystal laughed. "Yes, 'that'. We have to start planning this. It's going to be a big event. King Flavian has ensured that it will be a national holiday."

Markus huffed, "I think everyone is going overboard. It's a wedding, they happen every day."

Shio, Crystal's father, answered, "Not really. Both of you're famous, especially you, Markus."

"Besides," Fiona added, "after all the troubles this nation has been through since the Hallond incident and now this Dark Pearl situation, something to celebrate would be nice."

Markus nodded. "Fair point." He held Crystal's hand. "It's just that this is our day. Our wedding."

Crystal gave him a little kiss on his cheek. "Don't worry. The wedding can be for everyone to celebrate. The honeymoon will be just for us, trust me."

"About the honeymoon," Shio asked, "where are you planning on going?"

Crystal answered, "King Flavian has offered us the use of his private yacht, which will take us out to some islands near the Port of Pearls. Vacation spots used by the rich and connected."

Markus added, "Flavian's family has a private retreat that is normally only used by the governor to escape all the work of running the city. Should be a nice place for us just to be together."

"Sounds wonderful," Fiona said.

Markus asked, "So, what was the big discussion about location? I thought we were planning on having it at Thendor?"

Crystal answered, "That was just Flavian's idea. We haven't really settled on a location."

Margaret immediately said, "We should have it in the Valley. It's large enough for all the guests wanting to attend."

Fiona shook her head. "But, we want to have it in the court of the Blue Forests. It is the largest open courtroom in all of Gallenor, and very elegant."

Thomas was shaking his head. "I still think we should hold it at Thendor. The palace is perfect and the square can hold all the overflow guests."

Shio grunted, "But the city will still be under reconstruction. I say we have it here, at the college. Both kids are graduates of the college, so are we, and it is a nice place. There is plenty of room in the plains for all the guests."

Margaret huffed, "But, where would they stay? In tents?"

Thomas argued with his wife, "Where do you think they'll stay in the Valley? We don't exactly have a lot of Inns."

All four parents argued back and forth about the location, and none asked the bride or groom for their opinions on the matter.

Markus leaned over and whispered, "Wanna get out of here?"

"Think they'll notice us leave?"

Markus shook his head. "Nope. Come on." He slowly slid his chair back and stood with Crystal. They stealthily step away, and their respective parents were never the wiser.

They walked through the reception crowds, each taking a moment to acknowledge someone who greeted them. It was nice that most of the guests were friends of Markus and Crystal, so this situation was much more comfortable than others. Finally, they saw the happy couple standing near the table where gifts had been placed.

"Steffen!" Markus grabbed Steffen's hand and shook it. "I see that you changed. Wearing a shirt for longer than half an hour bothers you?" He noted the bare chest of this beefy man.

Steffen snorted, "A half hour, my butt. I was up at four in the morning getting that stuffy outfit on. I don't see how people always wear all that clothing. I guess after all these centuries of dressing like this, I'm too accustomed to it."

Donna told her husband, "Don't you ever stop being accustomed to this. I like what I see."

He flexed his chest. "For you, anything."

Crystal was giggling. "You sound like Treb."

Steffen frowned. "Why?"

"Oh, Treb is shirtless all the time; he likes to show off his chest. He makes up excuses if you ask him, but he likes people looking."

"But, there is so much to look at," Donna said.

Markus was deep in thought for a moment as he stared at Steffen's bare chest. "I'm curious about one thing."

"What's that?"

"You once told me that your muscular body was due to that tattoo and a spell on you. But, that spell was broken and the tattoo is gone. Why do you still have this body? I mean, even Treb isn't this muscly and works out daily. I haven't ever seen you work out."

Steffen brushed his hand over his thick forearm. "I've thought about that, too. I think it's a gift."

"Gift?" Crystal found that curious.

"Yes. When I first got that tattoo three thousand years ago, my single objective was to get this body. The person who gave it to me gave me that tattoo and set off an amazing and wild series of events, putting me in the center of a prophecy and eventually this war. Now that's all over, I think the blessing of this body, the whole reason I was after all that tattoo, is left. I'm not indestructible anymore, I can be injured, but I have the body I wanted from the beginning."

Markus smiled warmly. "I'm just glad you're still with us. I'm happy for the both of you."

"Oooh, look! They're bringing out the cake." Crystal pointed to a line of students following the chief baker from the school. They carried a large, five-tier wedding cake adorned in traditional Gallenorian wedding colors: blue and pink.

"I guess it's time to cut the cake and open gifts," Steffen said.

Donna was about to leave when she noticed a funny look on Markus's face. "What is it?" she asked.

He grinned. "I just realized something. Steffen is my great great great...well really great grandfather. And, you married him, which makes you my..."

She pointed a finger at his nose. "You call me grandma once, and I'll turn you into a rodent."

"You wouldn't dare!" Markus pretended to be offended.

She sneered at him. "I have a lot of secret potions at my disposal... and don't you forget it."

Crystal came back and pulled on Donna's arm. "Come on, it's time to cut the cake."

The crowd gathered and celebrated the cake cutting, and the gifts were opened. Dignitaries had sent many gifts due to Donna being a member of the Dragon council. Finally, everyone gathered to see the happy couple off.

Markus and Crystal stood near the exit to the school, their parents near them. Kiin and Treb were also close by, holding their baby. Donna transformed into a Dragon and Steffen situated himself onto her back. Flying high, they took off, waving to the crowd below.

Crystal leaned in close to Markus as they both waved to their friends. She asked him, "So, do you think they'll live happily ever after?"

Markus laughed. "Yes. Even if bad things happen again in Gallenor, they will be happy with each other. And so will we."

POST SCRIPT: A GOLEM'S STORY

MARKUS flew far over the Barren Mountains, beyond the cities of the Shlan, and across the wastelands. It felt like centuries since he first flew this direction with Korvarsk, so much has happened since those days. It was here that he battled the fake leviathan and entered the Sea Fairy kingdom. This is also where he first met Steffen, who spent years among the fairies. Finally, he saw the coastline in the distance, and the ruins of the Lost Port.

"Why did Steffen ask me to come up here?" He muttered as he headed directly for the old port.

Flying low over the city, he couldn't find any sign of Steffen, or anything else living. Then he saw a strange sight, a large hole in the water's surface. It was almost exactly where he had faced that water leviathan before. Landing, he transformed back into himself and slowly approached the water, unsure if the Sea Fairies might take offense again and attack.

"Hello?" he called out.

After a few moments, a blob of water appeared near the hole and one of those tiny fairies looked at him and then dashed back into the waters. Soon after that, Steffen came back up, holding a large satchel.

"Markus, good." Steffen came out as casual as if he were just leaving his closet with shoes to put on.

"What are you doing?" Markus asked, painfully curious about all of this.

"Just gathering some of my belongings I left here." Steffen held up a bulging bag.

Markus asked, "Did you need me to help you? How did you get here? It's a long walk."

"My wife dropped me off."

Markus looked around. "Is Donna here as well?"

"She's fine. She wanted to stay, but I asked her to leave. I wanted to meet with you privately. And, I suppose I could get a ride back... if you don't mind."

"Not at all. What did you want to see me about?"

Steffen looked up toward a larger building. "Let's go over there. I'd like to see what's left of the old palace."

Markus, still confused, flew him over to the broken remains of an old palace. They sat in what could have been the courtroom, though most of the ceiling had fallen in, exposing the sky above. The large, open floor was littered with broken chairs, chunks of stone from the walls, and a few metal candle stands that had rusted beyond repair. Steffen spent a moment eyeing a larger chair that was obviously for the regent of this city.

"Okay, we're here. What's going on?"

Steffen pulled out a rock from his bag. "I told you that Tolen had a strange history."

"Yes, his mother was Alieth, but he died as a baby, but came back... I think." The story never made sense to Markus. He tried to make it clear in his mind, but the details were too confusing. Of course, Steffen had been vague about it, and somewhat sad.

Steffen sat on the dusty old throne, staring at the stone. "I hid a lot of truths from Tolen, always afraid of causing him pain. I loved him and maybe over protected him. I want to show you what happened and how he came to be the boy I raised. Do you know what this is?" He handed the stone to Markus.

Markus looked it over. "Not really."

"That is a heart stone. A special, forbidden magic from a long time ago. I saved it and collected the memories that I wanted to save in it. I think it's time I show them to you. Hold it close and concentrate."

"Heart stone? I... I think I know of that. It is ancient magic. I don't think Tolen ever dealt with one before."

Steffen, still presenting the stone to Markus, answered, "The magic of a heart stone was made illegal during my lifetime before I got the tattoo. However, not every nation in the ancient world followed that rule. They were still made. They are the source of power that creates and controls golems, creatures of magic that do the bidding of who created them. At least, most of the time."

"Then, how does this contain memories?" Markus was still reluctant to touch it.

"This is a special heart stone. Trust me, it will be clear once you touch it."

Markus held the stone and suddenly felt like he was falling into a dream. It wasn't entirely surprising, he often did this with memories from the Dragonwand.

POST SCRIPT: CHAPTER 2

"YAH!" A lanky man cleared a large rock in one leap and dashed across the sandy desert.

An enormous black bird shook the ground when it made contact. It threatened its attacker with a shrill screech.

The warrior, dressed in leather clothing, long duster, and wide-brimmed hat, showed no fear. With sword ready he rushed the bird. "You won't get away from me this time!"

The bird's beak and the man's sword clashed in a fight. The creature, looming high over this warrior, snapped at him with sharp motions.

"That's it, you stupid chicken! Get mad! Come on! Get real mad!" He stabbed and slashed with each word.

In one swift motion, the bird had him up in a mighty bite. It bit down with all of its strength. All the while, he hit it with his sword.

"OW! DAMMIT! YOU CAN'T... STOP!" He fought against its grasp.

It clenched down on him and spit him out, sending him sprawling across the ground.

"Dumb bird! That won't do it!" He jumped to his feet. "SHOOT ME! COME ON! DO IT!"

The giant bird flapped its wings once and took off, ready to escape this painful prey. Seeing his target leave, the man launched his sword in the air. The huge blade stuck right into the chest of the bird, piercing it at the lungs and going into an artery. The poor creature slammed back into the ground with a hard smash, then screamed again. Finally, it unleashed its most devastating defense, electricity.

The man didn't move. He opened his arms and lifted his head with an appeased smile. The gathered static from the bird's body came out in one bolt that was more powerful than lightning. The mans body took the full brunt of the blast. An explosion followed and hundreds of rocks rained across the area as he was dismantled. All that remained was a single, red, beating heart stone. The bird stopped only when it died.

Just then a horse with no rider came running across the desert. It skidded to a stop right at the heart stone. Looking around frantically, he gasped and gently pushed the red glowing stone with his nose.

"Well, Cole, you did it," the horse spoke. "You got that overgrown crow to destroy you. Now, let's see if it lasts." The tone of this strange horse was hardly sympathetic.

Night had fallen over the desert, and billions of stars scattered across the crystal-clear skies. The horse occasionally glanced at the beating heart stone, but he spent most of his time watching the skies and enjoying them.

"What's that?" the horse said, looking up as a deep thrumming sound echoed across the vast expanse. A huge airship flew overhead, its propellers spinning where sails would be if it were a sea-faring vessel. The ship was painted in deep blue tones, with cobalt blue glass on most of its windows. Gold gilded the surfaces of the railing and masts. The horse watched in intense amazement. "That's no ordinary ship; that's a royal cruiser. I wonder what it's doing out here."

The rocks around the beating heart stone rattled and began to move. At first, they slowly scraped across the sandy surface. Soon, they were rolling, and some even flew through the air. They gathered around the heart stone, covering it. First, it was a pile, and then a flash of red magic filled it. They became a man, sitting there coughing. His body did not look like a pile of rocks, but that of a lanky, rough man with five o'clock shadow and a disgruntled sneer on his face.

The warrior who slew the bird knelt on the desert ground, dusting his pants off and checking his hat.

"Well, Cole, it didn't work," the horse said.

Cole, the warrior, stood and walked over to the horse. "Obviously. And where were you, Val? That bird tried to get away three times. I had to run through this hot desert for nine hours, and my horse is nowhere to be found."

"I was right behind you. You were so set on dismantling yourself that you left me in the dust. And, my name is Valiant."

Cole scoffed. "Just because the wizard who made you gave you that glorious name doesn't mean you deserve it. I'll call you Val."

"I do deserve it!" Val protested.

"You're a big coward; everyone knows it." Cole checked some of the packs on the saddle.

Val huffed and looked away. "Would a coward have stuck by you for three hundred years? I've been through a lot of crap carrying your scrawny butt all over this Empire. Even out to this distant colony."

"And you run at the first sign of danger."

"Look, I'm not the one trying to get himself killed. Unlike you, I want to stay in one piece for a few more centuries."

Cole found a dagger in his stuff. While he checked the edge with his dirty thumb he said, "When you get to be eight hundred, you get tired of being around. I've been through five wars and watched our empire nearly tear itself apart during the last one. I'm really tired. Golems were never meant to stick around for so long."

"I know, I know. You've told me. But, unlike every other golem I've ever seen, you can't be destroyed. You just keep coming back together." Val cocked his head. "Watcha doing with that knife?"

"Gotta get the eye out of that bird before we head back to the city. If I want to claim the bounty, I gotta prove I killed her."

"Ew, that's gross."

"Just be glad this isn't like that mountain spider nest we were hired to clean out back on the mainland. That potion maker paid us to carve up all the spiders for their spinners. I spent three months cleaning goo out of my clothes."

"Okay, I didn't need to recall that. I'm gonna throw up."

Cole sauntered away, muttering, "You can't; you don't eat."

***

Cole and Val walked down the tall cobblestone streets of the port city. This was called New Dawn Port, as the sun rose over the ocean facing the city. The day was young, and the streets were just beginning to fill with vendors. This city was the most beautiful place on the northern coasts of the land—at least, that's what Cole thought. Compared to him, this city was new. But after eight centuries, everything looked relatively new. This colony was established over a century ago when Alanor decided it was time to expand. Alanor was the land the wizards came from, it was the home of Steffen and the first Merlins.

Five snake-like people came rushing by with a cart full of supplies for deep sea fishing. The Shlan built the original port city that was now this new colony of Alanor. The ancient Shlan name of this port was Thal'shu'ski, but it was changed when they handed ownership over to Alanor.

"They're in a hurry," Val muttered.

Cole said, "They're Shlan, they are always in a hurry. Fastest people I've ever met."

"Not faster than me."

Cole rolled his eyes. "I'm not racing you against one of them again... I can't stand hearing you whine when you lose."

"Lose!"

The sun crested the distant horizon, its early morning rays glistening on the gentle waves of the bay.

Cole spent a moment gazing out over the ocean.

Val noticed this and nudged him. "Nice morning, eh?"

Cole gave his horse a sneer and moved on. "Seen it all before."

"Aw, come on. You were enjoying that... don't deny it."

"I don't have time to enjoy another sunrise. I want to get paid for this." He patted the bulging sack carrying the huge eyeball of that bird.

"Still gross," Val muttered. "Anyway. What's the big hurry? Not like anyone else is going to claim the bounty, unless more demon hawks are terrorizing the desert outside the city."

"It ain't easy walking around with a thing like this. Bothers people."

At that moment, a small boy ran up to Cole. "Mr. Cole! Mr. Cole! You're back!"

Though Cole's expression didn't change, he did stop for the child. "Morn'n, Trevis, just got back into town."

The boy was about to snag Cole in a hug when he stopped and jumped back. "Oh, what's that smell."

Val replied, "You don't wanna know, kid."

Trevis asked, "What are you doing today? Can I come with you?"

Val said, "A piece of advice, kid, find out what we're doing before asking to go with us. It's pretty boring."

"I like going with you," Trevis said.

Cole shrugged. "We're just heading for the local palace to speak with a magistrate. Have to collect on a bounty. Nothing fun."

The boy's eyes widened. "The palace! I want to go."

Val frowned. "You've seen the palace before. I know they let kids in on several occasions for tours."

"Not the palace, the ship. The big ship that came in this morning. It's so amazing. Please can I come! Please!"

"Big ship?" Cole frowned and looked out across the city toward the palace.

The aft section of a large airship could be seen from behind the back of the main building.

Val noticed the same ship that Cole was staring at. "Oh, right. I saw that thing coming in while you were scattered over the dirt. Just some big snob from the capital."

"I wonder if they have a wizard with them," Cole whispered.

Val gave him a funny look. "I doubt it."

"If they came in from Kelder Keep or Kirador, they might have a wizard with them."

"Only one way to find out," Val said. "Hop on; it's a long walk across the city to the palace."

Cole had a foot in a stirrup when Trevis grabbed his leg. "Wait! Take me with you."

Stepping back onto the street, Cole gently pushed Trevis away. "I can't. I don't know what I'm doing. Besides, I would have to tell your parents where you're going. I don't have time. This... uh, thing I have to turn in will smell much worse quickly if I don't get it to them. Just go and play with your friends."

Trevis backed up and nodded. "I will. Maybe you can show me the big ship and the palace later."

"Uh, sure." With that, Cole got up on his horse and trotted down the street toward the palace, leaving a teary-eyed child behind.

Once they were out of earshot of the boy, Val said, "You might have told him goodbye or something. If you find a wizard and they can end your spell, you'll never return. That boy really likes you."

"Trevis is a good kid. I don't know why he sticks to me so much. I wish he would find someone else. Maybe I should go back... No, I shouldn't."

"Oh, don't tell me the stone faced mercenary has a heart," Val teased.

"Shut it."

"Don't deny it. You act all gruff and mean and focused on your work. But, deep down, you care about people. Otherwise, you wouldn't help everyone out so much. Plus, you wouldn't be fighting with yourself right now about leaving that poor child without a friend."

Cole scoffed. "First, that boy probably has loads of friends. Second, it's not because of my feelings, it's just logical. To explain to a ten-year-old boy why I want to be destroyed would be impossible without telling him I'm a golem. Golems are illegal now. I don't want to cause that much trouble for us and him. No, it's better if I just disappear. He'll live. Right now, we have a mission."

POST SCRIPT: CHAPTER 3

COLE stood before a magistrate's desk in the main office of the palace. The plump fellow in charge of paperwork was currently checking the recent listings.

"Yup, here it is. One Demon Hawk reported over the wastes. Terrorizing farmlands near the Gnome lands." He looked up from the scroll of paper. "Do you have proof that you actually killed this creature?"

Cole plopped the cloth bag with the eye in it on the desk. It made a sickening slosh when it hit. The magistrate immediately covered his nose. Cole announced, "Right here. I got the eye. Nasty, but proof that this monster is dead."

The magistrate grabbed a stick and carefully pried open the top to look inside. With hesitation all over him, he looked down at that eye. "Okay, that's proof. Please, get it out of here."

"What about the bounty?"

The ill-looking man quickly handed Cole a bag of coins. "That's more than the bounty, but I'm willing to pay extra for you to get that out of here."

"What do I do with this eye?" Cole picked up the money and the eye, one bag in each hand.

"Take it to be destroyed."

Cole held up the eye, which made the poor magistrate flinch. "Only a wizard can nix something like this. Demon Hawks are filled with a lot of dark magic."

"Then take to Merlin. He's here, and he's a wizard."

Cole's eyes bugged. "The Lord Dragon... is here?"

"Yes. He's meeting with the governor now."

"Thank you." Cole bowed and left the office.

He walked through the large, modest governors palace. Every place he went, people wrinkled their noses or simply left in a hurry. He was stopped by a pair of guards who protected the main audience room. Cole explained his situation, and with encouragement from the odor, they agreed to tell Merlin about him.

A new feeling stirred within him: anticipation. He had never met the Lord Dragon. In all his life, he couldn't recall a moment when he had seen this person. As a lone warrior and sword for hire, he had spent so much time that he had never really encountered Merlin or any of his court. This would be something new, and it was a strange feeling for an eight-hundred-year-old person.

Cole assumed it would be a long wait; Merlin's time was limited. However, in moments, the guard returned and was escorting him inside the audience room.

The first person he recognized was a woman, the governor of New Dawn Port. She was a dark-skinned lady who drew a lot of attention from men. She was a good leader whom Cole respected.

The man next to her looked out of place in this room. He was large, wearing only pants, and had well-defined muscles. On his upper right arm was a strange tattoo. It was the absence of a wizard that made Cole frown. A small delegation of Shlan courtiers quickly bowed out, all of them covering their noses as they left from the scent of Cole's bag.

Cole paused and simply waited.

Governor Ketrix finished checking over a scroll and then looked up. "What is that awful smell?"

Before Cole could explain, the beefy man beside her said, "That's the stench of rotting dark magic."

She sneered at Cole. "What are you doing in here?"

"I was invited. I came to see Master Merlin about this." He held up the bag.

The beefy man waved at him. "Then, by all means, come see me. I want to dispose of that immediately."

Cole's expression was genuine shock, which was abnormal for him. He slowly approached this man. "Are you a wizard?"

The man smiled. "Yes, I happen to be a wizard."

Ketrix laughed. "He's not just any wizard, this is Master Merlin, the Lord Dragon, head of the Dragon Council and leader of the united lands of Alanor and Kirador."

Merlin smiled and said, "But, you may call me Steffen. Now, Governor, if there is no further business. I would like to speak with this one alone. We have magical matters to tend to. Plus, I suspect the smell will get much worse when I have to examine this object."

Ketrix rose from her seat and bowed to Merlin. "Understood. I look forward to dinner this evening on my carrier. The sunsets here are nearly as glorious as the sunrises." She flashed a flirty smile before leaving with her entourage of guards.

After that, Merlin waved the other guards out of the room. When they had gone, he commented, "Good, I get tired of being watched all the time. Now, let's move on to the matter of this item."

Cole paused as he looked at his man closer. "I've seen you before, no that's not possible. That was a long time ago."

"Oh, do tell?" Merlin playfully asked.

"I guess I saw an ancestor of yours, close to eight hundred years ago, when I was first made. He was leading the wizards in the Great War...He was a the fire dragon, head of the Dragon Council."

"Yes. That was a terrible war. The Heart of Darkness had gained control of several dragons, and we had almost lost everything. But, we prevailed."

Cole cocked his head. "You... can't be that old."

Merlin leaned over. "And you can't be a golem... but here we are."

"You know I'm a golem?" Cole had never been spotted as a golem before in eight centuries, save when the few saw his body crumble and the reassemble.

"Yes. I could sense it when you came in. I've been around golem magic before; it is distinct. However, most magic users today don't know the difference since golems were banned three hundred years ago from all lands, even the Aliki."

Cole nodded. "That's part of why I'm here. I need to speak about..."

Merlin held his nose. "If you don't mind, let's deal with this first. Please, open the top of the bag." He reached over and picked up an impressive staff with a dragon's head on top.

Cole opened the bag with the withering Demon Hawk eye. "Here, it's pretty ripe about now. Good thing my sense of smell is lousy."

Merlin held his nose with one hand and nudged the bag open a little farther with the other. He cast a spell with the staff and the eye disintegrated into a fine black mist. He directed it into a bottle and quickly corked it. "There. I can study that later." Releasing his nose, he took in a deeper breath. "Ah, that helped a lot. The scent should go away quickly." With a casual wave of his wand, a gentle breeze stirred in the room toward the open windows.

"Why did you keep that mist? It's just magic residue."

Merlin set his staff back down. "I'm here because there has been a surge of dark magic creatures in this new land. The northern wastes are littered with shadow wolves, demon hawks, and imps. I'm concerned about the surge."

Cole gasped. "The corruption. Is it here?"

Merlin somberly nodded. "Yes. The corruption has nearly claimed all the lands back home. I can't find a reason behind its expansion and why it's showing up here."

"Is that why the Shlan delegates are in town, to talk about this?"

"Yes. The corruption has already impacted the gnome lands, but now it is spreading south into the Shlan Empire. They are only seeing the beginning of it, but if it isn't stopped now, it could claim their lands as well."

"I can't help you with that."

"Don't worry about it. That's for another time," Merlin said. "I'm curious about you. What's a golem doing here? And, from what you've already said, you're very old. After the Aliki war, I didn't expect to see any golems anywhere. Not only is their construction banned, but those around were destroyed."

"I can't explain why I'm still here. I was created a long time ago—eight hundred years ago, to be exact. Conventional means can't destroy me for reasons that baffle everyone. The spell on my heart stone is formidable. I wish to be disassembled and even attacked that foolish bird just to see if it could do the job. I was convinced that dark magic constructs that big were strong enough to end me. But I was mistaken."

Steffen rubbed his chin. "Interesting. Let me see your heart." He held up his hand and Cole suddenly became a cloud of rocks. His physical form vanished, leaving his heart floating in midair momentarily. It soared into Merlin's waiting hand. He peered into it. "Fascinating... truly fascinating," he muttered. Releasing it, the heart floated back into the cloud of stones, and Cole reappeared again.

Cole, a little wobbly for the experience, said, "Well, what did you see?"

"Your heart... it's not normal. I've seen all sorts of heart stones. Most basic ones are made with simple magic. Those golems are hardly more than tools. The more advanced ones used the life force of a sacrificed animal. This gave them the ability to think and act more human-like, but still not human. Yours is much stronger than that. The energy in it is unique."

"What, so they sacrificed a more powerful animal?"

"No." Merlin paused for a moment, deep in thought, then finally nodded. "It has to be. Yes, your heart stone was enchanted using the life force of a human."

Cole's mouth hung open. "Wait, so a human was sacrificed in some kind of dark ritual?"

"No, that would never work. This life force is willing. Whoever did this gave their life force for the stone. I suspect that you were crafted when someone was near death. They allowed their life to be used for this. That must be it. I've seen this kind of magic before, but it is rare and illegal."

"Why would it be more illegal than other forms of sacrificial magic?"

Merlin answered, "The prospect of crafting powerful, death-proof soldiers would be too great. Imagine vast armies of powerful golems who cannot be destroyed. No, this is too terrible to think about."

"All I know is that I want to die. I want to end this life. I have been around for eight centuries. My purpose is over; my work is done. I wander this world hoping to find my end, only to see more strife, unhappiness, and darkness. Please, master wizard, cast a disenchantment and relieve me of this burden of life." Cole went down on one knee.

"I need more."

"What?"

"I need to know why you have decided to end this life? What struggle has given you this strong desire?"

Cole was silent for a long moment; it took time to say, "Long ago, when I first arrived in this new land, I worked for a family here. They were kind and good to me. They knew what I was and kept my secret because I posed no threat to anyone. But as time passed, the people grew old and passed away. The children I helped bring into this world died as elderly people. I never aged. I made friends with them and came to understand love in ways I thought a golem could not. When the last member of that family died, I realized it was time for me to go as well. Learning to love is wonderful, but understanding true pain comes with it. It is painful to live forever when no one else can. No one can comprehend how terrible this is?"

Merlin's gentle smile had faded into remorse. "I understand this as well. I have outlived loved ones for centuries, including my wife. I continue on because I know there is a purpose for me. However, if I had no purpose other than to go on, it would be unbearable pain. I will try to grant you your end." He lifted his staff and raised it, asking, "Are you sure about this?"

Cole stood firm. "Yes. Please, just do it."

The last thing Cole saw was Merlin swiping his staff to the side and the world darkened. Then, he opened his eyes again and looked at Merlin, standing before him. By the light in the windows, he realized time had passed. "What... what happened to me?"

Merlin was smiling with a curious frown. "It didn't work. The magic in you resisted my disenchantment."

Cole was at a loss for words. Finally, he yelled, "DAMN!"

"Calm down."

"Calm down! I finally find a wizard, not just any wizard, the most powerful wizard in the known world. And even he cannot break this curse."

"There is a reason," Merlin quietly said.

Cole was caught off guard. He slowly turned his head to Merlin. "What?"

"While you were disassembled, I could hear your heart beat. I was wrong. This is not a person's life force at the end of their life. This is a child—a very young child who was near death. Your creator was a parent of this child. The force of life in you is strong and desires to live. That desire is so strong it is keeping you from breaking apart."

"You're telling me a parent sacrificed their child for my heart?" Cole was horrified.

Merlin paused before answering; he was suppressing a deep pain. "No. This is a parent who watched their child near death and couldn't bear the thought of losing them so young. They used forbidden magic to create the heart stone, allowing the child's life to continue in a golem."

Cole frowned. "Wouldn't this parent want to have their child? If they wanted to save them, why create a basic warrior golem with it? I don't remember being a human child or anything like that."

"My best guess would be that it failed to work as the parent hoped. The stone didn't give the golem the mind of the child, just life. But that child, mind and all, still lives in your heart. I truly have never seen this before. It is amazing. You harbor in you the lifeforce of a child who wants to live, wants to grow up."

"What do I do about this? Will this child keep me alive forever?"

Merlin sat back down. "I cannot say. But, I sense that you have a choice in this."

"What do you mean? If I had a choice, do you think I would have worked so hard for so long to find a way to end my existence?" Cole's temper boiled hotter with each word.

Merlin said, "It isn't a choice of ending you, but of accepting life."

"That doesn't make sense!"

"There will come a time, a single moment, when you are truly ready to let this life pass on, that Cole can end so the life inside him can be happy. How and why, I am not privy to that foresight. But, you will meet your end, of that I am certain"

Cole huffed. "You know, I can't stand wizards. You are a cryptic type of people."

Merlin laughed. "I know. It comes with old age as well. You may be eight hundred; I'm over two thousand. We all have a purpose and will see it when the time is right, even you."

Cole reached down and picked up the now empty sack. "Thank you for your time." He bowed out and left to retrieve his horse from the stable master.

POST SCRIPT: CHAPTER 4

"THEN that stable boy, the one with the cold hands, wanted to check my teeth. He was all worried that I wasn't eating enough. Like I look thin or something." Val complained, which was normal after he had to stay in a stable.

"Just be glad they didn't want to experiment on you. Remember that wizard who wanted to study you?" Cole muttered.

"Sure. But, next time they poke places I don't want them to, I will kick that stubby boy right in the..."

Cole yanked on his reigns. "Shut it. We're here."

They walked into the blue light district, named due to the color of lamps used here. Though each district was colored to help people find their way, the colors have now come to mean status. The red light district was the market streets. The yellow light district was the nobles and royalty. The green light was the wealthy elite. This blue light district was the poorest area. However, one would be hard-pressed to find a livelier place. Even though people were used to Val talking, it made some of the older stock nervous.

Cole tied Val to an old hitching post and then pulled out the bag of gold. He approached an old woman sitting outside on the steps of the row house. "Nani."

She smiled her old wrinkled face at him. "If it isn't my handsome friend. My, you haven't aged a day since I first met you. I wish I had your blood in my veins." She said this each time she saw him.

Cole knelt and pulled out a handful of the coins. "Are you well?"

"Oh, my knees hurt. I can't see too well, and my memory is bad. Oh, and my knees hurt."

Cole took her hands and pressed the coins in. "Here. Get some medicine for your knees."

She looked at the ten gold coins. "Oh, my. How sweet of you. How did you know my knees were hurting?"

He laughed. "A good guess. Also, you might ask the doctor about a memory potion."

"I might just do that."

Cole looked up at a younger woman standing at the top of the steps. This was Nani's granddaughter. She noted the needs and the money so that it would be used and not forgotten. After a short nod to her, Cole moved up the street.

He handed out small portions of his gold to people along the way. Toward the end of the street, he was met by the representative. Each district had one for the court and came from the district they represented.

"Master Cole." He bowed.

Cole bowed back. "Nolund. How are you today?"

"Distressed. First, I must thank you for what you have done. Don't think your good deeds have gone unnoticed."

"Just remember, don't tell anyone about it. I don't want to have people begging me for money. I only give what I have, I don't run a mission or anything."

Nolund smiled. "I respect that. On a sad note, I need your help."

"My help?"

"Yes. I can't offer you much money, but I must hire you."

Cole frowned. "For what? Hunting a dangerous animal around the Blue district?"

"I only wish it was a dangerous animal. Take a look around, do you see something odd here?"

Cole glanced around. "No... wait, yes. Where are all the kids? These streets are normally bustling with kids playing."

"It seems that at night, someone is coming and capturing them. They are sold to slavers in the port."

"Slavers! But, how could slavers be in our port? They are not allowed in any part of Alanorian lands, even the colonies!"

Nolund saw the people unsettled by the commotion, so he spoke more silently. "Yes, slavers are illegal and keep their business well hidden. Our problem is that they are taking our kids."

"Have you alerted the magistrates?"

Nolund nodded. "I have done my duty as a representative. But, it seems that our problems come behind many other issues. They promise to inspect the ships but won't spare extra security to watch our street at night. I come to you not as the representative, but as a citizen worried about the children around here."

Cole nodded. "I will do what I can. I'll patrol the streets at night and keep an eye out. And I won't take any money for it."

"No, please. We do have a fund gathered." Nolund lifted a small bag of coins.

Cole smiled and pushed the hands down. "No. I probably gave people some of that money. Keep it; give it back to them. I will help because it is the right thing to do."

"Thank you." Nolund was almost in tears.

"COLE!" a happy voice yelled out.

Nolund smiled. "Oh, here comes one of the lucky children."

Cole smiled at first but became worried. He knelt to greet the boy. Trevis ran right into him, stumbling over his own feet. Cole held him by the shoulders and looked at his bruised face. "Trevis, what happened. I left you this morning and you were fine."

"I... uh... fell. I'm okay. Do you have any gold for us?" he asked insistently.

Cole shook his head. "Sorry, I just ran out."

"Oh, please, anything. Silver pieces, something!" Trevis' eyes started watering.

"Don't cry..." Cole tried to console the distraught child, but Trevis was already bawling. A hand nudged Cole's arm and he saw that little bag of coins Nolund had offered. He reluctantly pulled out five gold pieces and then put them in Trevis' hand. "Here, please, take them."

Trevis, blubbering, looked at the gold. "Oh, thank goodness. Oh, this is real money."

"Yes. Now, go home and clean yourself up. Get something cold on that bruise." Cole stood.

Trevis ran with all of his might back down the street.

Cole looked at Nolund. "That was... unusual. I've never seen him so upset."

"Me neither. But his life has been hard since his mother died a few months back. It's difficult to lose a parent at his age."

"Trust me, no one understands the pain of watching people you care about die more than I."

***

Nighttime came and Val harangued Cole as they returned to the Blue light district. "So, not only did you fail to be disenchanted, but now you're working as a night watchman for these people. Didn't you say something about not getting too attached to people?"

Cole stared straight ahead as he walked, holding Val's reins. "I'm not getting attached. This isn't about individuals like our old family. This is just a street of scared people. While in one piece, I can do something to help them. So, I'm helping. Do you have a problem?"

"Not really. This is going to be boring, standing around all night. But, we've done worse. You talked with that port security guy. Did he say that any of the ships were suspect?"

Cole shook his head. "No. They don't think any of them are slavers. A couple have been in port for a while, but they checked out."

"You and I both know that the security can be bribed."

Cole nodded. "I know. They wouldn't willingly let a slaver bribe them, but if they are convinced it's just dodging port taxes on merchandise, they'll look the other way and never realize they have failed to catch a slaver."

Val nodded his big head. "Then, why don't we go out there and do some inspecting of our own? You know, break in a few ships, bust some heads together. Get things done. Not just stand around a dark street and dawdle."

"I'm not a vigilante. I'll help and if I find those pirates, they're gonna wish..." Just then they both heard a child screaming.

The voice in the distance kept screaming, "I'm sorry... no... don't... please, I'm sorry."

"That sounds like Trevis," Val said.

Cole was already running. "It does."

"Hey, don't rush off without me. I'm your transportation." Val was right behind him.

Cole came to an abrupt stop, which nearly made Val run right over him. The terrified boy was down the dark alleys and was just screaming in fear. Suddenly, the screaming stopped when a harsh hit with an object could be heard.

"GET ON!" Val yelled.

Cole launched himself into the saddle as Val dashed off down the dark, winding alleys.

They chased the shadows and hints of sound around this town's buildings and back alleys. After a long run, they wound through the Blue and Green Light districts. Soon, they were out onto the docks.

"Look!" Val called out.

In the distance, a man carrying a child over his shoulder walked down the dock to a ship. Another figure came down the plank and approached the man.

Cole pulled back on the reins. "Wait, looks like they've been spotted."

Val smiled. "Hey, great. It's a security guard. He'll... Wait a minute. What's he doing?"

Cole leaned over and watched the blurry silhouettes interact. The figure from the boat handed the guard something, then the guard simply turned and walked away. The sound of squeaking leather in

Coles's hand indicated how hard he was now grasping the reins. "That... that... traitor."

Val didn't require any encouragement, he ran right at the guard. "I'll get him, you get to that ship."

Cole waited for the right moment. Just as Val was going to turn up a street to follow the guard, he jumped off and tumbled with a practiced roll. He went from the roll into a run in seconds, not losing momentum.

Val ran up the cobblestone street for the guard. The man turned with a wide-eyed expression at the sound of those hooves on his trail. No sooner did he see Val's approach, he found two hooves flailing at him. He was knocked to the ground. Again the horse reared up and then stomped back down. One hoof broke his spear in two, the other broke his shin.

"Yah! My leg!" he screamed.

Val leaned over and nearly growled, "Be glad I'm letting you live."

The guard was visibly shaking while he held his shattered appendage.

Cole approached the pier and slowed, knowing he had the upper hand. He always had the upper hand since he was made of stone and couldn't be killed.

The husky voice of the ship captain could be heard. "He's no good, he's dead."

"He ain't dead, just knocked senseless. Struggled awful bad."

The captain lifted the boy's head. "Too much blood, you hit him too hard. No, he's no good. If he comes around, maybe. My buyers..."

"Wait, I heard something." The man carrying Trevis turned around and saw Cole slowly approaching. "Damn!" He tossed the boy over the side of the dock and jumped in, swimming for all his worth to get away.

Cole realized that Trevis would drown and dove in after him. He got to the child and swam him to shore. Briefly checking, he found that Trevis was still breathing but badly hurt. At the same time, the boat was now leaving the dock. He knew the ship had been at this port for a month, and they would still be on board if they had the children. He had to do the right thing. "I will come back for you." He whispered and then ran down the dock again with all his strength.

The captain and his crew watched the lone warrior dashing across the dock. They were snickering and mocking him as they moved too far away to be reached. Or, so they thought. Cole reached the end of the pier and made a huge leap into the air. He crashed into the ship's deck and tumbled repeatedly as he careened toward the mast.

Sitting up, Cole found five blades pointed at his face. The captain, not brandishing a weapon, was laughing. "What did you think yer doing here? Huh? Far as I see, I can either sell you as a slave, or chop you up into chum."

Cole, without any fear in his eyes, stood. "Tell me one thing, do you have the missing children here?"

"Why does it matter?"

"Answer me! Do you have them?"

The captain shrugged. "What if I do? They're just street urchin worth money to the right buyer."

"Trust me, they are worth much more than you. I will return them to their homes now. You can surrender or I can take you down. Your choice."

His crew chortled. The captain shook his head. "You don't even have a weapon."

"Sure I do." Cole ran right into a sword wielded by a woman. The blade went all the way through, the tip coming out his back. He smiled and grabbed the girl by the throat. With a twisting motion, he spun around, threw her over the side of the ship, and pulled the blade from his body. Now he was staring down a crew of stunned, terrified pirates. He flashed a wicked smile and whispered, "Who wants to go next?"

Val was escorted back to the docks by a new security guard who had arrived at Cole's request. Upon reaching the docks, Val noticed a whole squad of security directed by the chief magistrate. They led several pirates away in chains, most mumbling about a demon on their ship. Additionally, more guards were tending to the numerous children who had been rescued from the depths of the ship.

Cole knelt next to Trevis with Govenor Ketrix and Merlin. "Cole! Cole!" Val hurried over.

Ketrix looked up. "Oh, Valiant, I was wondering where you were."

"I was caring for a creep who took a bribe for..."

"We know," Ketrix interrupted. "Cole has explained that. We have arrested several men already."

Val looked down at the boy while Merlin had his staff over his head. Val asked, "Is he...dead?"

Merlin looked up with a smile. "No, but he was in bad shape. A few healing charms have brought him around. Rest and recovery is what he needs. Someone should take him home."

Cole reached down and gently picked up the child. "I'll take him home. I know where he lives."

As Cole stood, Ketrix stood with him. "We can't thank you enough."

"Just make sure it doesn't happen again."

Ketrix bowed her head to him. "I will do my best. I just wish we had caught the culprit kidnapping them."

"He jumped into the water and swam away. I'd have got him if he hadn't thrown Trevis in as well."

Merlin asked, "Was he one of the pirates?"

Cole shook his head. "I don't know. He didn't talk like them, they all had a unique accent. Besides, he jumped into the water and swam toward the city. No, I suspect he is a resident here, making money kidnapping children."

Ketrix said, "I'll set an alert tonight, and we will search this city high and low for this kidnapper. We will also be investigating our security force for taking bribes. If you will excuse me, I have a lot of work to do. She left to speak with the head magistrate.

"I'd love to help her," Val said. "I enjoyed kicking that jerk, but I wouldn't mind kicking a few more."

Merlin helped secure the child on Val's back. He patted the horse. "A fine steed. I haven't seen a golem of this quality in a long time."

"Wait, you know?" Val replied.

Merlin nodded, "Yes. But don't worry. Just take good care of this child."

Cole took Val's reins."We will. Goodnight." He walked his horse back up the street.

It was going to be a long walk back, they had to take it slow and steady.

Cole approached the house with Trevis cradled in his arms. The boy was coming around and made a few noises. Cole knocked on the door, but no one answered. Finally, he was able to open it and walked right in.

"Hello!" he called out.

A man entered the room, a towel around his neck and a robe on. "Who are you? What are you doing in my house?"

"I'm a friend of Trevis. He was hurt." Cole turned with the boy in his arms.

"Oh... my goodness. What happened?" The man didn't sound too worried.

Cole found a couch and placed the boy on it. "He was kidnapped by someone stealing children. I don't know what he was doing outside this late, but I rescued him. He was hurt pretty bad, but a wizard helped heal him. He should be all right."

"Oh, uh, thanks. I'll look after him. Do you, uh, need payment or anything?"

"No. Just be sure to let him rest and don't let him go outside tomorrow and run around."

"Sure. I'll do that. Now, I have to get ready. Early job."

Cole gave the man a funny look and then tipped his hat to him. "Good morning." With that he left the home.

Outside, Val met Cole and eagerly asked, "So, was his father happy?"

"Not really. Something about that didn't feel right. Maybe I'm just on edge after all this."

Val walked with him back down the street. "It has been an interesting night. We busted a slaver operation, caught some corrupt guards, saved that boy's life. Pretty good work. I think we deserve a rest."

"You know we don't need rest, you're just lazy and... did you hear something." Cole stopped and looked back. They could hear voices coming from Trevis's home.

Inside Trevis home, the boy opened his eyes and found an awful sight above him. His father was looking down at him. "No!" he screamed.

His father grabbed him by the arms and pulled him up. "You're gonna shut up and never tell anyone what happened."

"I won't! I'm going to run away!"

"Where?" His father slapped him across the face.

Holding his head from the pain, Trevis trembled. "I won't run. I promise, I won't tell anyone you tried to sell me."

His father struck him again and again. "No, you won't tell anyone. You won't tell anyone ever again!" He continued hitting his son while Trevis wailed in pain and fear.

Suddenly, the door of their home burst open and Val smashed clear through it. Cole came running in, grabbed the father by the hand, and twisted his arm so hard that it snapped at the shoulder. The man screamed in pain. Cole threw him aside and came down to the child.

Trevis was still, his eyes open and his body shaking. What little he was breathing suddenly stopped.

Cole held his hands. "No, no, please don't die. No."

"I'm get'n out of here!" His father, holding his injured arm, attempted to escape.

Val swung his head at the man and slammed him against a wall. He went down in a slump, knocked of his senses. "You ain't going anywhere, jerk."

Cole felt the boy's chest. "I can't feel it! I can't feel it! He's..." he tried to say it, but couldn't put the words together.

Val looked around quickly. "I'll get... someone. Merlin, I'll find Merlin!"

"It's too late," Cole whispered. "If any life is left in him, it won't be there much longer."

Val's lips quivered. "Oh, Cole... he was so young. He... was a good kid."

Cole put his head on the boy's chest, holding his hands together in one of his. "I can't take this, I can't watch another person die. Why do I live forever when a child has to die? BY THE HAND

OF HIS OWN FATHER! WHY!" He was screaming at the world more than anything else. He wept, for the first time in his life, and he could cry real tears.

"Cole?" Val watched as his body began to glow.

Cole whispered, "I would give my life if it would mean this child could live."

There came a great thumping from inside Cole. His body emanated a brilliant glow that was not unlike the glow that came from his heart stone. Each time it pounded, it grew in intensity.

"Cole? What are you doing?" Val backed up.

Cole looked up. "It's my time. This is it."

"I don't understand." Val called out.

Cole looked at his faithful friend. "Thank you. You were always the bravest, most loyal friend I had in all my long life. Goodbye."

Suddenly, the throbbing energy exploded outward, sending a wave of light that spread out of the house and across the city. It came again, and then again, each a beat of his heart exploding with all the magical energy within. Throughout the city, people woke to an amazing light that permeated the world for just a short few moments.

Val had to close his eyes as the light was so great. When he opened them again, the light was gone, the pulsing energy had vanished, and the world was back to normal. Next to Trevis was a pile of stones. The heart stone rested on the boy's chest, which no longer glowed.

Trevis opened his eyes, his face bruised and blood still on his mouth He saw Val standing over him and felt that stone in his hand. "What happened?"

Merlin stood at the edge of his balcony in the guest suite of the palace. Those waves of light passed him, and he slowly opened his mouth in awe. He held up his hand and the staff he carried appeared in it. With a great leap, he jumped over the railing and out of the five-story tall room. Midair, he transformed into a Dragon and flew high into the sky.

Val sat in the middle of the living room with Trevis' father firmly held under his horse butt. Trevis was still laying on the couch holding that heart stone with a curious frown.

"This... is me," he said quietly.

Val repeated himself, "no, Trevis, that's a rock, a magical stone. You are not it."

"Trevis?" He looked at Val with a confused expression, then nodded, "Yes, that's my name... but it isn't."

"You're worrying me, kid."

Trevis' father woke to find his legs pinned down by the horse. "GAH! What's going on! OW OW, WHY CAN'T I MOVE!"

Val stomped a foot. "Shut up!"

"Get off, get off!"

238

"Oh, shut up! Don't make me sit on your head!"

Just then an odd shadow flew over the house. It was huge, and looked a little like that demon hawk. People outside screamed and ran.

"Oh, crud. Just what we need, one of those dumb birds," Val muttered.

An enormous thump came outside the window, the shadow covering the house. Instantly, that shadow vanished as though it had disappeared.

"Father?" The boy sat up.

"Father?" Val whispered, not sure why he would say this.

Merlin stepped in, holding his Dragonwand.

"Who are you! Get this horse off of me!" Trevis' father yelled and shoved on Val's backside.

"Be quiet, that's Merlin!" Val stated.

"Merlin?" Trevis' father gasped, with a lot of dread now filling his eyes.

Merlin hadn't noticed any of this exchange, he was staring at the child on the couch, "I... I don't believe it."

The boy looked up and squinted. "I know you."

Merlin came over and knelt near the pile of rocks, taking the boy by the hands. "What... what is your name?"

"I don't know. I feel strange."

"Hey, leave my kid alone!" Trevis' father yelled.

239

Val said, "Your kid! HA! You tried to sell him and then almost murdered him. My best buddy... gave his heart to save him."

"What are you talking about your stupid animal! I wouldn't hurt my kid."

Merlin looked back at the man and stated, "He is not your child! Not any longer!"

"He most certainly is!"

"Father," the boy said, looking at Merlin. "Yes, you... you are my father."

Merlin nodded. "Yes. I am your father, you are my son, Tolen."

POST SCRIPT: CHAPTER 5

TWO weeks passed and Val was led into the main courtroom of New Dawn Palace. The guard directing him had to explain to five other guards that the horse was requested by Merlin. A young man with a special shovel and pale followed behind, though it was unnecessary.

Inside the courtroom was Master Merlin and Governor Ketrix.

"Greetings, Val." Ketrix smiled.

"Your ladyship." He bowed his head.

She waved a hand and two guards escorted Trevis' father into the room. He was bound in chains and dressed in prison rags.

"What is that scum doing in here?" Val asked.

Ketrix said, "By the law, two witnesses must be present to confirm murder charges. Merlin can stand as a witness, but you are the only witness. It is unusual to ask an animal to be a witness, but seeing as you are enchanted and as smart as any human, you may stand. Is this man the culprit behind the murder of his son and the kidnapping of many others?"

Val looked at the man. "Uh, the kid's still alive, no thanks to this man."

Merlin stated, "I have confirmed to this court that this boy is not Trevis, but my son Tolen."

"Oookay?" Val frowned and looked back at the culprit. "If you're asking me if this jerk beat his son to death, then I'd say yes. And, he was the one who was taking all the others."

"Good enough for me." Ketrix signed a parchment and stood. "By the laws that govern the Alanorian Empire, you are hereby formally charged with murder, kidnapping, slavery, and abuse. You will stand trial. Take him away!"

The guards pulled the man back out of the room.

"Is that what you needed me for?" Val asked.

Ketrix was still signing paperwork as she answered, "Not entirely. Master Merlin wished to speak with you."

"Oh?" Val looked at Merlin.

Merlin told Ketrix, "I wish to speak with him alone."

"Oh, of course." She picked up her paperwork, handed it to a scribe, and got up and left.

"Everyone else, please," Merlin stated and the guards left the room.

Finally, it was just the two of them. Val said, "Um, okay, what do you need?"

Merlin got up and approached Val. "How have you been?"

"Me? As well as any golem horse can be, I suppose."

Merlin patted Val on the neck. "I doubt that. You've been wandering around the city for two weeks. You have nowhere to go and have lost your best friend."

"Best friend, that scrawny jerk. Ha." Val suddenly blubbered out, "Of course, he was my best friend. We've been together for centuries."

Merlin patted Val on the neck some more. "I'm sorry for your loss. But, your loss is my gain. What I wanted to talk to you about is what happened to Cole. You deserve to know the truth."

"What do you mean?"

"Cole had a very special heart stone that kept him alive for centuries longer than any normal golem. You see... that heart stone was filled with the life of my only child."

"What?" Val stepped back.

Merlin said, "I had an interesting encounter with the Elder Oak back in the homeland. It told me to come here, that I would find something I had been looking for. I assumed it was answers about the current corruption crisis. I never imagined it would be this. When I first met Cole and tried to help him dismantle himself, I sensed something in the heart stone that brought a spark of hope. However, after eight centuries of looking, I believed it was just foolish hope of an old father. When I felt him give his power over to the boy, I knew that soul."

"So, you created a heart stone? Why?"

"Yes, I am his creator. My only son, born to a woman I loved dearly, was not well. He lived for a very short time. I tried to save him using forbidden magic and placed his soul in a heart stone. It failed, and I kept the stone to prevent it from being misused. I believed my boy was dead. This was nearly a thousand years ago."

"Wait, wait, wait. Cole was only eight hundred years old."

"True. But, the heart stone wasn't used to make a golem long ago. It was stolen from me, and I thought it lost forever. I never knew it was used to make a warrior golem, and I certainly never thought it would come back to me in this way. Cole carried my son, my baby, to me and when the time came, he passed on and gave the soul to a living child."

"So, the boy who I saw wake up, the one you took with you, is not Trevis?"

"There is a tiny spark of life left in him from Trevis, but in reality the soul in that body is my sons, Tolen. He has some memories of Trevis' life, he even has a few memories of Cole's life, but otherwise, he is my son."

Val asked, "Is he like a baby now?"

"No. It's more like he has a terrible case of amnesia. He can function as a young child but is learning who he is again. I am going to teach him, raise him, and love him as I wanted to for so long."

"Why tell me all of this?" Val said. "My friend is gone forever, I am all alone, the last living Golem... I think."

Merlin nodded. "I doubt there are any others. I am telling you this because you deserve to know, for Cole's sake. He gave his life so that my son could live. He wanted to save Trevis, and I did not want you to think he failed."

"But you say Trevis is dead."

"True. And in a way, he is. But he will live on in my son."

"I guess that's good."

Merlin guided Val toward the large open windows overlooking the ocean. He asked Val, "What will you do now?"

"I don't know. I never thought the day would come that Cole and I wouldn't be together. I was created for him by an old Aliki mage. I've only known life with him around. I honestly thought he wouldn't ever be destroyed and that I would go first."

"If you don't have plans, I would like you to stay with me and help watch over my boy. You can also tell him about his savior, Cole. I'm sure your adventures would be great stories for a young man to listen to."

"The ones I'm willing to talk about. The stuff we've gotten into is crazy!" Val laughed.

"I'd love to hear them."

Val sighed, "I love talking about them."

"Then you'll stick around?"

"Sure. Why not. If you don't mind a talking horse."

Merlin gave a short laugh. "Trust me, I've missed having a talking animal around."

"Huh?"

"Never mind." Merlin and Val watched a large ship come into dock. A quiet moment broke when Merlin said, "There is just one thing. Please, don't tell him all of what I said about how the heart stone was created. Let him think he is just Tolen, my son."

"Why?"

"I don't want him hurt. Trevis had a hard life, and Tolen's mother died a thousand years ago. I love him; I love my son, and I don't want him to hurt because of all that has happened. I just want him to grow up having a happy life."

Val asked, "What about his old memories of Cole and Trevis?"

"To him, they are just a part of his foggy past. He doesn't understand that they are memories; to him, they are just vague dreams that he can't explain. They will eventually become a part of his personality, and he will forget that they were odd memories."

"You asked me to tell him about Cole?"

Merlin said, "True. Spin your amazing adventures as exciting tales. Entertain him, inspire him, but, let's keep some of the truth hidden for his sake."

Val spent a moment and then nodded. "I will keep the secret. I too want that boy to be happy. No child should have to suffer what he has been through."

Just then the room doors opened and a guard held Tolen by the hand, "Um, sorry, Master Merlin, this boy wanted to see you."

"Let him through, he's my son." Merlin calmly answered with a big smile.

Tolen was released and he bolted across the room and grabbed Merlin in a big hug. "Daddy!"

Val watched this exchange of hugs and smiled.

Markus sat back, looking at Steffen with new eyes. "That... was amazing."

Steffen took the stone from him. "Tolen never truly understood his origins. He never knew who his mother was and he didn't know that he wasn't born naturally to me. I am ashamed of how much I kept from him, even though my reasons were for his benefit. I wish I had dared to tell him the whole story. Part of me feared he might look at me differently if he knew."

"He would have," Markus said. "I can't say how, exactly. However, I know he would have loved you no less for knowing this. What happened to Val?"

Steffen gave off a little laugh. "Val lived for another fifty years. He was a good friend and a loyal guardian of my son. However, he was an ordinary golem. When his time came, he fell apart and ceased to exist. I saved his memories in this heart stone, so the story of Cole and Val would not be lost."

Markus said, "In a way, your son lived two lives. He lived as Cole, doing amazing, wonderful things for eight centuries. Then was reborn as Tolen, bringing the son back to his father."

Steffen put the stone back in his bag. "Come on, let's go home. I have a life to live as well, and so do you."

Markus asked, "Will you tell me about your adventures before you had Tolen? How you got that tattoo, where you came from. So little is known about the ancient wizard lands."

Steffen quietly looked out across the sea, in the direction of the ancient lands. "That is a long story, one day I will tell it to you. I promise."

ABOUT THE AUTHOR

Daniel Peyton is a fresh author whose talents includes, writing, sketching, and dreaming out adventures in faraway places that he seeks to bring to paper. He lives in East Tennessee where he draws a great deal of inspiration from the unique landscape. He has been featured in short story e-zines as well as flash fiction blogs. Legacy of Dragonwand: Book IV is the fourth installment in the Dragonwand Saga. Outside of authoring books, Daniel is an award-winning cook, artist, and embroiderer. He is a distinguished member of the Sigma Alpha Iota, and often can be found teaching classes at his church. Before he began seriously devoting himself to becoming a published author, he spent over ten years traveling the country as a member of the Miyagi Ryu Nosho Kai dance school, performing Okinawan classic and modern dances.

Follow Daniel@

Website: PeytonPublications.com

MORE BOOKS FROM DANIEL PEYTON

LEGACY OF DRAGONWAND BOOK I

OUT NOW

LEGACY OF DRAGONWAND BOOK II

OUT NOW

LEGACY OF DRAGONWAND BOOK III

OUT NOW

LEGACY OF DRAGONWAND BOOK IV

OUT NOW

LEGACY OF DRAGONWAND BOOK V

OUT NOW

LEGACY OF DRAGONWAND BOOK VI

OUT NOW

Cosby Media Productions™

Entertaining the Mind, and Inspiring the Soul

www.cosbymediaproductions.com

www.ingramcontent.com/pod-product-compliance
Lightning Source LLC
Chambersburg PA
CBHW052026020726
47501CB00004B/1271